A Very Coastal Christmas

Camille Cabrera

Dedicated:

To the creative interested in making a better world. Reality can be inspired by your most wonderful dreams, if only you have the courage to do.

Introduction:

Belladonna (Blue) Wickam spends her days painting and her afternoons walking along the sandy shore of her quiet coastal town— the perfect routine.

When the body of a famous environmentalist winds up in the nearby wetlands, Blue takes it upon herself to comb the sleepy shoreside for clues. She's tossed into the deep end as the storm of the century threatens to make landfall just before Christmas Eve. Will she be able to collect all of the clues before the weather spins her cozy life into chaos?

Blue thinks she can handle everything except the stubborn and objectively handsome out-of-town lawyer insisting on offering his help. For some reason, Blue can't shake the feeling that she just needs to look at the information from a different perspective. A perspective that might come too late if Blue doesn't hurry.

Chapter 1

Grains of sand whirled down from the top of the dunes and licked against Blue's exposed feet. She steadily walked over the slopes as her pink-painted toenails winked at the afternoon sun between steps.

She lifted her head and admired the sea as it leisurely lapped against the shoreline. It was unusual to have such a pleasant day so late into the winter season. Blue wanted to make the best of it as she walked over the sporadically placed dunes and crept along the outskirts of the lively wetlands positioned just in front of her two-story coastal home. Three generations of Wickhams had lived in that house. If Blue had her way, three more would be able to enjoy its splendor.

The wetlands was a rarity positioned between Blue's home and the beach. When she was feeling lazy, she liked to take a little-known shortcut through the freshwater habitat. The walk from her home to the center of town took less than 20 minutes. Blue held the brown envelope close to her chest as a strong wind swept her blonde bangs to the side. Her tanned skin displayed a smattering of freckles accumulated over 30 sea-loving years.

She needed to get to town before Amanda left the art gallery for lunch. While the chore wasn't time-sensitive, personally handing over a few updates about her latest collection of oil paintings was the perfect excuse to stretch her legs.

Blue navigated the same beach that the women in her family had traveled for decades. She liked to think that her toes had a way of touching the same grains of sand as her ancestors. Grounded in the past and poised for the future. A sleepy future, of course. Nothing of any consequence ever happened in Shoreside.

Waves licked against the distant dunes while a few freshwater birds ascended into the sky. White egrets moved deeper into the wetlands surrounding the shore. The wetlands were somewhat of an oddity. They were a place where freshwater hugged saltwater. If Blue remembered correctly, there were only a handful of coastal wetlands left in the west.

Distracted, Blue ambled deeper into the wetlands. She strayed from her usual path as she carefully navigated the mud and avoided a few potentially prickly plants.

Nature's excited chatter lulled to a dull murmur as Blue entered the sacred space. The scent of sea salt mixed with dewy marshes greeted her senses.

A pair of sneakers poked out from a mess of green vegetation. Blue rolled her eyes as she walked closer. The high schoolers were at it again; always throwing parties out of the purvey of prying parental eyes.

Blue's steps faltered as she noticed the sneakers were attached to legs. A body tilted headfirst into the water as feet pointed to the sky. Blood rushed into Blue's ears as she quickly spun in a circle. She didn't need to check for a pulse.

Her shaky fingers grabbed her phone from the back of her linen pants and dialed the local police station. For once, she remembered to take her phone. Maybe that was the problem. When did anything good happen when Blue had her phone?

"Hi, Sheriff Lennox. This is Belladonna. I found a body in the wetlands. No, I'm not joking. No, it's not a bird photographer sitting very still. Look, Sheriff Lennox, do you want me to call Linsy and tell her that you're ignoring my concerns?

Okay, I'll see you in a few minutes near the dirt road."

She sucked in a deep breath and tried to commit the sight in front of her to memory. Blue was one of the few people that could never look away. She needed to look at every part of the world because it made her feel safer than closing her eyes.

An irritated hiss escaped her lips, "This is what I get for bringing my phone."

Blue hung up her phone and looked down at her toes. The paint appeared a shade or two duller than before. She turned in the direction of the dirt road as she accidentally crunched the envelope squashed beneath her arm. Perhaps the tides were changing around Shoreside.

Chapter 2

Steam rose from the surface of Blue's cup as she stared out the window. Fog rolled through the center of town. The heavy crawling clouds usually brought a calming quality to the coastal bungalows and sleepy shacks, but today the brume whispered unnerving secrets. Blue's mind kept taking her back into the wetlands. As a child, she played games and raced through the murky waters. The fond memories battled against her recent rattling discovery and created tension in her heart. She felt conflicted.

"How are you doing? Sorry, that's a stupid question. You just saw a dead body."

A ghost of a smile danced along Blue's pouty lips as she looked at her cousin. A statuesque woman with cropped locks and severe chopped bangs slid Blue's tote bag onto the opposite seat. People in Shoreside rarely got out of bed before ten in the morning. Luckily for Blue, her cousin ran the only coffee shop in town. Its doors opened early for the wayward traveler or overachieving jogger.

Blue rubbed a hand over her tired eyes. "I still can't believe someone died in the water."

"I can't believe you found a dead body!"

Blue slunk lower in her seat as she cautiously dared a glance at the couple seated only a few tables over. Two curious pairs of eyes skittered over Blue's face before they quickly retreated to their section of the coffee shop. Mercifully, no one else was in shouting distance.

An elaborately decorated Christmas tree offered some semblance of privacy. Blue did her best to angle her body behind the festive decor.

Better.

Melinda didn't bat an eye as she kept her attention glued to Blue's wiggling figure. While Blue usually loved her cousin's bubbly, bold behavior, this didn't feel like the right time to have the same vocal range as a microphone.

Oh, well.

Melinda tapped the side of her cup as she pressed, "You didn't respond to my text messages."

"Oh, sorry. I left my phone on the side table near my front door."

"You're always forgetting your phone. One day you're going to need to use it."

"Well, I brought it with me once and look how that turned out. What a mess. Hopefully, I won't need it again for at least a million years; long after this gets sorted. Sheriff Lennox said he would let me know if he had any more questions. Do you know if anyone from town is missing?"

Blue wanted to add that she didn't recognize the man but the words refused to leave the safety of her throat. She coughed and took another sip of her drink as she tried to navigate a conversation she highly doubted anyone knew how to begin.

Melinda sniffed as she reached into Blue's tote bag and pulled out the latest copy of the Shoreside Press. The front of the local newspaper showcased a black and white photo of last year's Christmas Market. With the next Christmas Market less than a month away, the town was moving at full speed to cover every inch of Heart Street with the festive decorations. Every lamp post was wrapped in a generous layer of green garland and light mingling of morning fog. Given the paper's front story, it was safe to say the local news didn't know about the recent body.

Blue fussed, "That doesn't look promising."

Her cousin took a much more optimistic approach as she shrugged one shoulder and quickly leafed through the content. Melinda's brows pulled together once she reached the editorial mentions placed near the end of the paper. Not even a peep.

"The editorial staff usually put the paper together the day before. Maybe they'll mention something tomorrow."

"Yesterday's news, read today."

"Very funny."

Melinda shrugged half a shoulder as she loudly sipped her whipped cream-covered beverage. She stared over the mountain of sugary white swirls and teased, "I'm just trying to lighten the mood."

Blue hummed in agreement as she gripped the side of her mug. She took a sip of her cooling cappuccino and sighed. Maybe she'd learn something more in the morning. She reached into her pocket and pulled out her phone. Blue scrolled over the recent Shoreside news updates and found a combination of Christmas Market-related news and seafood advertisements. Nothing out of the usual. Which given the circumstances, felt unusual.

"I'll speak with Sheriff Lennox tomorrow and see what he says. People just don't wind up dead in the middle of the wetlands."

Melinda's tongue darted out and whipped away the white mustache above her upper lip. She stared out her shop's window and mumbled, "I'm sure the mayor is throwing a fit."

"Why would you say that?"

"A dead body right before the Christmas Market doesn't exactly scream tourist attraction of the year. This town makes half its seasonal revenue during the holiday season and the rest during the summer. If this gets out, the entire town will be sunk."

"Maybe you're right."

Melinda tossed her head back and laughed, "I hope not. That would be so morally bankrupt. We're a small town, not a big city government. I'm sure we still have some standards."

Blue wrinkled her nose. The topic felt too dark. What if Melinda was right? What if the mayor had specifically stopped the story about the dead body from running in the paper? A shiver of dread raced down the back of Blue's spine. She wanted to focus on something more upbeat. The Christmas Market had never sounded like such a wonderful event to fixate on. Soon, the streets would be filled with eager Christmas shoppers and plenty of visitors. It was one of Blue's favorite Shoreside traditions. The coastal town sure knew how to celebrate. For obvious reasons, this year's upcoming festivities were shrouded in gloom.

Not one to shy away from a hard question, Blue decided she needed to do some investigating of her own. She looked at complex problems like different brush strokes against a wide spanning canvas. Each stroke worked together to create a masterpiece. Perhaps Blue was sitting too close to the canvas to be able to see the larger picture.

Melinda talked about her latest adventure sailing along the coast while Blue tried her best to pay attention. Two cups of coffee later, she felt energized and ready to take on the rest of the day. Blue stood and walked over to the front door.

She was about to leave but a colorized poster caught her eye. Display homes and towering apartment complexes covered the paper tacked to the local announcement board.

Blue read over the paper and asked, "What's this?"

"Oh, some fancy developer wants to put a new luxury apartment complex near the water. The town seems pretty divided about it."

"Why didn't I know about this earlier? This looks like it's going to be built right next to my home."

Melinda rolled her eyes as she popped her hip and groaned, "They're really rushing the job. I think the mayor is trying to get the project approved while offering the developer a bunch of discounts. Something about increasing town profits, blah, blah. Greedy windbag."

Blue balked. She quickly looked around the coffee shop as mirth danced behind her eyes. She mumbled, "You can't just call the mayor a windbag, can you?"

"Well, I just did. Besides, we all know it's true. He loves the job because he gets to dress up as the boss. Howard wasn't even the first pick for the position. It's too bad Myna Sage ended up withdrawing from the mayoral race. I bet Howard did something sneaky to make sure he would win."

"I wouldn't be too worried. The world has a way of balancing out. You just love a good conspiracy theory."

"And you love to paint life in black and white. Literally. Would it kill you to put some color into your oil paintings?"

Blue huffed, "Thanks for the coffee, Melinda. See you soon."

The door clicked shut as Blue ambled onto the street. Tendrils of fog danced around her ankles but she didn't give the gloomy weather much mind. It would disappear in a few more hours. She thought back to the poster proudly displaying soulless luxury eyesores and laughed. How could a house be a home if it didn't have any soul? Blue now had two things added to her to-do list. She needed to speak to the police chief and attend the upcoming town hall about the development. Blue didn't mind change as long as it left people better off than where they started. Her gut told her that wouldn't be the case when it came to the pending boxy eyesores.

Given the surprising speed and underhanded nature of the massive development, Blue had her suspicions about the positive impact of the luxury apartments. Still, she wanted to learn a little bit more about the project before she gave in to her initial dismay. Blue knew she tended to get stuck in her ways. She liked to create black-and-white paintings and hated using her phone. But that wasn't the point. When it came to the larger town, some change could be good, right?

Chapter 3

For a person who usually went with the flow, Blue felt like her recent endeavors had her fighting the current. She had called Sheriff Lennox first thing in the morning but her call had gone straight to voicemail. The latest edition of the Shoreside Press hadn't mentioned anything mysterious about the wetlands. Most of the paper was dedicated to the upcoming Christmas Market and told attendees random snippets of information like where to find the best parking. The silence on Sheriff Lennox's end felt even more disquieting.

With a huff, Blue zipped up her cream-colored coat and wrapped a heavy scarf around her neck. She stomped out her front door and walked the mile trek to the one-room Sheriff's Department. When the biggest crime in town tended to be bike theft, the funding for anything bigger than a quaint department felt a bit silly. Still, a few updates to the building could only help. Today was one of those days where Blue wished the crooked wooden sign outside of the department could at least look a little more official.

The scent of freshly brewed coffee and powdered donuts greeted her senses as she shoved open the department's door. Sheriff Lennox stood off to the side as he donned a crooked sparkly party hat. Linsy, his secretary, cheered her lungs out after blowing out a single candle pressed into a pink-sprinkled donut.

"Is it somebody's birthday?" Blue stumbled over the words as she looked at the scene in front of her.

Linsy pushed up her thick-rimmed glasses and laughed. Her bubbly nature was constantly at odds with Lennox's grumpy energy. Linsy pointed at a box of donuts and explained, "No! We're celebrating. It's Sheriff Lennox's 20th anniversary of joining the department."

"So we're calling it a celebration? I would call this a hostile work environment," Lennox moved away from the wall as he walked over to Blue. The smile twitching at the corner of his lips betrayed the amusement hiding behind the forced gruffness in his voice. Try as he might, he couldn't hide the mirth dancing behind his eyes.

"Congratulations, Sheriff Lennox."

"See, I knew people would see it my way. Aren't you glad I put together a party for you?"

Sheriff Lennox looked over at Linsy as she excitedly moved around the space, practically dancing in her work-appropriate kitten heels. The sternness in his features softened as he huffed, "I plead the fifth."

Linsy handed Blue a sparkly paper plate and asked, "What can we help you with, Blue?"

Chapter 4

Talk about a mood killer. Blue hadn't wanted to bring up the subject but she worried she wouldn't have the courage to come back. She needed to know if the death was a horrible accident. It was now or never.

To Sheriff Lennox's credit, he'd kindly thanked Linsy for the donuts and promised to continue the celebration after answering Blue's questions. Unfortunately, his answers were less productive than searching in the middle of the night for seashells along the shore without a flashlight.

Blue understood it was an ongoing investigation, but his answers were so vague that it almost felt comical. To be fair, Sheriff Lennox had said that the mayor wanted it handled as discreetly as possible. Blue made a mental note to tell Melinda she was right. The mayor did have a say in the confidential nature of the investigation. Maybe Melinda's other theory about trawling for blue lobsters wasn't as crazy as it seemed. That was a mystery for another day.

After speaking with Sheriff Lennox, the only thing Blue had to go on was an accidental slip of the tongue. Sheriff Lennox had accidentally mentioned that the body belonged to a famous environmental activist. It wasn't much but at least it was a start.

The walk to the local Post Office helped organize Blue's thoughts as she scrambled to put together her next move. She wanted answers. For some reason, it bothered her how the mayor had instructed Sheriff Lennox to keep quiet about the murder. To Blue, it felt almost like trying to erase someone from the fabric of Shoreside's history. It didn't sit right with Blue that someone could be walking along the bustling streets one day and drowned in the isolated wetlands the next. The wrongness roiled her belly as she pondered what to do next.

The intentional silencing of the death made the situation feel more sinister with every passing moment. Why all the secrecy if it was an accidental drowning? Blue was practically bursting with unanswered questions.

A sudden force crashed into Blue's face and pushed her to the ground. Her oversized bag flipped and all of her belongings toppled to the sidewalk. Brushes and paints littered the ground. The concrete looked as if a crafts store had thrown a wayward going out-of-business sale.

Dazed, Blue looked up from her awkward position on the ground and realized someone had pushed the Post Office's door open without looking through the tiny window first. Two shocked chocolate orbs locked onto Blue's ocean gaze. A man in his mid-thirties cocked his head to the side as he looked down at Blue. His large hand pressed against the Post Office's door as his hulking form stood frozen in the entryway.

From the look of the man, he was new to town. His clean-cut suit and freshly shaved jaw hinted at his big-city lifestyle. It also helped that Blue knew every local by name. She would have made it a point to remember the handsome stranger's name.

Blue licked her lower lip and sighed, "You have to look through the tiny window. You can't see people walking on the street without looking through the window."

Blue's words freed him from his stupor. He awkwardly lowered his weight onto his haunches as he attempted to meet Blue's eyes.

A deep voice asked, "Are you okay? Do you feel like vomiting?"

The handsome stranger reached out a tentative hand. Blue snorted as she extended her right hand and carefully placed it inside the newcomer's warm palm. She looked into his perceptive eyes and teased, "I don't have a concussion if that's what you're worried about. My dignity took a beating, but my body will live."

A tentative smile crept along the stranger's face. He swiftly collected her belongings and handed over the items. After a minute, he pulled Blue back onto her feet. His movements were so elegant that Blue barely had time to register the change. She leaned forward and accidentally gripped his forearm as she tried to regain her balance. Realizing her overstep, Blue awkwardly coughed and moved away. Her flustered mind cleared as she built a meager amount of distance between their bodies.

"My name is Belladonna, but my friends call me Blue. I don't recognize you from around town."

"Belladonna, like the plant. Do you think the saying that people grow into their names is true?"

"Why? Are you afraid of my beautiful but potentially deadly nature? If so, you should probably call me Blue."

Usually, Blue wasn't exactly the flirtatious type. No, she usually made it a point to avoid overt pleasantries. Her paintings and long walks along the beach were more than enough for her.

She enjoyed her unchallenged perspective of life. Blue appreciated her routine filled with silence and beautiful art. Over the years, she'd become comfortable in her even-tempered solitude.

Something about the honey-colored orbs practically staring into her soul elicited a more fiery approach. Maybe it was the jolt to her head making her tongue looser than usual. Either way, Blue planned to seize the moment.

"It's nice to meet you, Blue. I'm sorry about the circumstances. I guess I can't pretend to be a local after knocking you over with the Post Office's door. My name is Charlie."

Blue smirked, "Beginner's luck."

She teasingly shook her unsent package in the air and hefted her large tote higher onto her shoulder. After a minute, she hesitantly rubbed the blossoming bump on the side of her head.

"Can I get you any ice?"

Blue laughed, "Do you have time?"

"I always have time for the victims of my foolishness."

"So you make a habit of knocking people over wherever you go?"

Charlie chuckled, "Would it help if I said you were the first?"

"Maybe."

His warm gaze flitted down to the large package tightly secured within Blue's grasp. Charlie pulled his brows together and asked, "Would you like to hand that over to the Post Office before we get some ice for your head?"

"Yes, I don't want to upset a customer."

Charlie arched his brow, "A customer?"

His eyes curiously traced over the package and Blue had to fight to keep a smile from overtaking her face. Charlie couldn't see the small black and white oil painting designed to mimic a stormy day off the coast of Malibu nestled inside of the package. It was one of her more intricate smaller pieces. The custom commission was worth a pretty penny. Luckily, she'd wrapped the piece several times over. The Malibu masterpiece would be fine.

"I'll tell you all about my customers over a hand towel and a baggie of ice."

Blue kept her words vague. She had a feeling Charlie would be able to put together the clues. He'd just helped her pick up several brushes and oil paints from the ground. Surely, he'd connect the dots.

Instead of commenting further, Charlie laughed, "I accept your terms and conditions."

"Now you sound like a lawyer," Blue teased as she walked through the door Charlie opened.

"You guessed it. Luckily, I never claimed to be something other than my chosen profession."

Blue grinned as she led the way over to the Post Office's counter. She tilted her head up and grinned, "My mother told me all about lawyers."

"Hopefully only positive reviews."

"Something like that."

Unused envelopes and bright festive wrapping paper lined the store walls. While a small town, Shoreside seemed to send out as many festive packages during the holiday season as it received. Luckily, Mr. McCulley made sure the building never ran out of celebratory ribbons and brightly colored packing materials.

Blue waved at Mr. McCulley and handed him the small package. He accepted the package and promptly returned his attention to Blue. Mr. McCulley took one look at the growing bump on Blue's head and gasped. He emphatically waved in the front door's direction and groaned, "We need to change the door. It keeps getting the best of newcomers."

Blue sighed, "It's okay, Mr. McCulley. No need to change the door when this happens every once in a blue moon."

Mr. McCulley escaped to the backroom. Blue observed Charlie as they listened to what sounded like the opening and closing of a heavy door. Charlie noticed Blue's inquisitive gaze and offered a small shrug. After a few minutes, Mr. McCulley returned with a small baggie of ice wrapped in a wad of clean tissues.

Blue gratefully accepted the ice. She winced as the cold bit against her irritated skin. The gobs of tissues did little to mitigate the frigid temperature. After a minute, the pulse racing through her injured head lessened to a dull throb. Blue's features softened as she stood on the tips of her toes and leaned across the counter."Thank you, Mr. McCulley. What do I owe you?"

Charlie quickly stepped into the conversation while Mr. McCulley weighed the package. He shook his head and interrupted, "Please let me pay. I need to apologize after messing up the local swing of things."

Mr. Mculley pretended not to hear Charlie and Blue as they squabbled over payment. Instead, the white-haired postal worker carried on with his day and swiftly processed Blue's order. After sending the package on its way, Mr. McCulley clapped his hands together and shooed them out the door.

"Are you sure?"

Mr. McCulley chuckled, "I make it a habit of picking up the tab for whoever gets hit in the face with the door."

Blue joked, "I guess I need to make it a point to wait outside the door whenever I need to ship a heavy oil painting."

"Sharp as always. See you around, Blue."

"Thank you, Mr. McCulley."

Charlie carefully looked out the window before he opened the front door. His eyes scanned the street for pedestrians several times before a satisfied look crossed his face. Charlie held the door and waited for Blue to exit.

"Thank you," Blue was about to say more but a loud ring cut her off.

Charlie checked his phone and his brows pulled together as soon as he spotted the name illuminated across the screen. Blue was too far away to catch the name but from Charlie's unhappy expression, it wasn't anyone he wanted to hear from.

She tried her best to offer him privacy but the effort was mostly pointless. His deep voice projected and it didn't help that he stood less than two feet away.

"Hello. Yes. I'll be there shortly. Thank you for letting me know."

Charlie ended the phone call and shoved his phone into the pocket of his tailored pants. He sent Blue a hesitant look. His thick dark brows pulled together as he tried to weigh his options.

Hoping to lighten the weight from his shoulders, Blue quipped, "Difficult boss?"

Charlie's shoulders sagged with relief as he agreed, "You have no idea. Could I take you to dinner as an apology? I'd hate to earn a reputation as the only person in town who doesn't know how to open a door."

"We can't have that. How about we meet at Nico's Eatery at around seven?"

"Perfect, see you soon," Charlie waved and quickly walked down the street. He towered over the rest of the crowd as he maneuvered to his car.

Blue forced herself to stop staring. She sucked in a deep breath and tightened her hold on her tote bag. The cumbersome weight helped to steady her nerves. As an artist, she loved keeping her tools close. Her portable oils and brushes made it easy for Blue to create masterpieces on the fly. She had hoped to find a little extra time in her day to craft a freehand image. Apparently, her day had other plans. She walked down the road and wondered how she would explain her online painting requests to a clumsy but well-mannered lawyer. Maybe she could playfully mislead him before finally telling him the truth. Was her career that obvious? Maybe. The paint splotches along her sleeves and permanently stained jeans tended to give her away.

Blue missed the pair of eyes following her movements from a distance as she cluelessly carried on with her day. For a small coastal town, the current around Shoreside seemed to be changing for the worse.

Chapter 5

Blue figured she had a few more minutes before she needed to start walking to town. A knock on Blue's front door beckoned her away from her favorite room. She stood on the tips of her toes and tried to see who was standing on her porch. Usually, she just flung the door wide open. Given recent events, she figured it was better to look. Well, attempt to look. Blue grumbled, she rarely used the peephole. The fact the stranger's face was too tall to be within sight did little to quell her nerves. Blue searched around for a potential weapon. The muddied sneakers near the door wouldn't do much good. She frantically looked around and grabbed a wooden broom. Something was better than nothing.

"Hello? Is this Belladonna Wickam's house?"

Relief filled Blue's chest. She recognized the voice from earlier in the day. Blue huffed and opened the door. Her gaze traveled up a tapered waist and broad shoulders before eventually meeting a well-sculpted face. Charlie donned dark blue jeans and a smart knit sweater. The sweater's warm color made his observant dark eyes pop.

A frown quickly troubled Charlie's features as he noted, "The door wasn't locked."

"I used the peephole."

"What's with the broom?"

Color crawled up the side of Blue's neck as she tried to save face. Deciding the best option was an honest answer, she huffed, "I was planning to clean a potential thief to death."

"Couldn't you see my face?"

Another awkward pause filled the space. Blue placed a hand on her hip and hummed, "No. The peephole is too high. I was about to wing it, but then you called out."

"Pepper spray and a small stool," Charlie's sharp gaze assessed Blue's door as if it was an offensive object. His fingers wrapped around something familiar and Blue instantly perked up.

"Is that my miniature painting kit?"

Charlie chuckled as he held it out. He scratched the back of his neck and admitted, "Yes. Mr. McCulley found it underneath the red bench outside of the post office. He made me promise to bring it right over to you. I thought about waiting for you to get to the restaurant, but then I wasn't sure if it was a small town custom to walk people to the date."

"The date," Blue's voice held a playful note as she eagerly accepted her miniature paints and placed them on her side table.

"Just stating the obvious for the record."

Blue laughed, "You like to make things clear from the start."

"Yes. It's probably why I decided to become a lawyer in the first place. Was it a special collection of paints?"

Blue looked over at her miniature monochrome oil paints and laughed. The sound rang clearly through the fresh ocean air while the hem of her cotton dress whipped around in the light wind. She jutted her chin out and pointed to the art supplies.

"I like to paint in black and white."

"I see. So you also like a certain level of clarity."

Blue added, "I don't believe in using shades of gray in my artwork if that's what you're saying. I don't even use color. My life is clear and straightforward; just the way I like to paint the world."

"Right, everything should have a clear answer. Does this mean people buy your work online and you ship it across the country?"

"Haha, yes. I wanted to keep you guessing about my career, but the wayward paint supplies gave me away."

Charlie teasingly narrowed his eyes, "I'm more observant than I look. It also didn't help that Mr. McCulley spoke to me for over 20 minutes about your artwork. He's convinced you're one of the most prolific artists in Shoreside. Do we have time to see a few examples of your work?"

Blue smiled as she stepped back and held open her light blue front door. She joked, "We aren't a busy town. Mr. McCulley just says that because I come from a long line of artists. Some people in town jokingly call us the Wickam Witches of Shoreside."

"Witches?"

Blue rolled her eyes, "People like to toss the word around when they can't understand the heart of a smart independent woman."

"That's some introduction. Now, I'd love to see the artwork produced by a Wickam Witch."

Blue laughed, "I think we can squeeze in a quick trip to my art studio."

Blue led the way and opened the door to her private sanctuary. Something about the motion felt oddly intimate. She usually kept the door closed whenever she had company. Melinda had only stepped foot into the sunroom a handful of times. For some reason, showing the room to Charlie felt right.

She padded through her art studio and admired how the light from the curved sunroom showcased her freshly drying oil painting. Unsurprisingly, it was another black-and-white image of the sea. This image captured the ferocity of a roaring black wave as it towered above a helpless ship. The painting froze the scene just moments before the vessel was poised to receive the impending blow. The inevitability of the ship's fate made the painting bittersweet. Blue stood back and appreciated how the waning light danced along the canvas.

She sighed and pulled her attention to the other artwork proudly displayed around the room. Over three generations of art filled the room. Blue could identify the artist simply by the way the brush strokes swayed. While Blue's mother had preferred concise slim strokes, Blue's grandmother had opted for broad, quick slashes. The energy within each painting always mirrored their creator's passion.

"I wonder where I fit in," Blue folded her cardigan over her chest and tried to spot any unique traits. For the longest time, she'd thought that her monochrome preference was her signature. Now, she wasn't so sure. What would happen if she experimented with color?

Charlie moved from one beautifully crafted scene to the other. Blue noticed how his eyes tended to hover on her works a little longer than the others. He gestured to Blue's latest work and asked, "You paint black and white coastal scenes?"

"Maybe I just haven't found a situation messy enough to warrant any colors."

"I guess it depends."

"Oh?"

Charlie leaned against the room's door frame as he continued, "Yes, what warrants color for you will likely not inspire another artist."

"Now you are really starting to sound like a lawyer. We better head over to

Nico's Eatery before we end up spending the rest of the night looking at contracts."

"I'll settle for looking over a menu."

Charlie's easy confidence made it easy for Blue to lightly press and poke. Blue was sure that she'd have a problem if any other newcomer showed up to her house unannounced. For some reason, she was willing to make an exception for Charlie.

"Ready to walk over?"

"Should you lead the way?"

"Sure, I know this town like the back of my hand. Oh look, a new freckle."

Blue kept her gaze on her left hand as she turned over her palm and jokingly looked at a supposedly new freckle. The two left the sunroom effectively doubling as an art room. Charlie walked down the porch and waited near the winding rock-covered path for Blue to lead the way.

He offered Blue his hand as she descended the handful of stairs. Charlie guffawed, "Great, the dad jokes will keep us company."

"Laughter feeds the soul."

Charlie groaned, "Hopefully Nico's Eatery will feed my stomach."

The sun glimmered in the sky as distant gulls called through the air.

Surrounded by chaos, Blue took a moment
to enjoy the calm before the storm.

Chapter 6

"If I ever look at another lasagna, it will be too soon." Charlie paid their bill and left a generous tip. His dark orbs danced with mirth as he pulled out Blue's seat and waited for her to stand.

"Nico's is one of the best places in town. I can't think of a better place to eat besides my own kitchen."

Charlie tipped his head to the side, "Do you like to cook?"

"No, but I do appreciate how close my kitchen is to my art studio. It's comforting to know that I have a creative outlet nearby."

"I see."

Christmas lights wrapped around countless miles of garlands winked in the early evening hours. Each storefront glowed with warmth. Blue particularly liked the handcrafted paper snowflakes proudly displayed around Melinda's coffee shop window. A few of the snowflakes were lopsided but Blue thought that the imperfection made the display more realistic. Too much perfection made art look fake. To Blue, the best art included wayward brushstrokes and a few wrinkled canvas lines.

"I forgot to ask. What brought you to Shoreside?" Blue kicked a small pebble off the sidewalk and watched as it toppled over the curb.

Charlie's eyes followed the movement. Eventually, his gaze returned to Blue's face. Standing made their height difference more obvious. While Blue didn't consider herself extremely small, she definitely struggled to see over a few counters around town. It was safe to assume Charlie hadn't experienced the same problem around town. As it stood, he had needed to duck to get into the older dining sections of Nico's Eatery.

His melodic voice pulled Blue back to the present. Charlie shared, "I'm here for work. I typically work remotely, but my boss wanted me nearby. The change in scenery is pretty nice."

"Where did you come from?"

"The East Coast. It's exciting to visit a California coastal town. The weather is so much nicer."

"It's foggy almost every day."

"You don't like the fog?"

Blue tried her best not to snort as she quipped, "I didn't say that. It's just difficult to appreciate the weather when every morning feels coated in a dark layer of gloom. But maybe you're right. Maybe I'm looking at the weather negatively since I'm in a rut."

"What's wrong?"

Blue stumbled over a small crack in the sidewalk once she realized her mistake. So much for being able to keep a secret. To be fair, Sheriff Lennox hadn't said to keep the mysterious death a secret. He'd simply said that the mayor didn't want any bad press circulating before the Christmas Market. Blue carefully weighed her options. She didn't want to lie to Charlie. Her gut found the town's general silence about the discovery of the body to be downright wrong. Why would the mayor try and hide something so big from the Shoreside community? Surely, friends and family members related to the person were already asking questions.

Before Blue could over analyze the situation, she went with her gut. She stumbled over her words as she explained, "I recently discovered a dead body in the wetlands. The authorities are investigating but it's really ruffled my feathers."

Charlie stopped walking. It took Blue a few steps before she realized that Charlie had stopped walking. She turned on her heel and sighed, "I know. It's not exactly the best conversation to end a date."

"You knew about a dead body and still opened your front door without looking through the peephole?"

Blue huffed, "That's not fair. I couldn't see. Besides, I knew it was you from the sound of your voice."

If Charlie wanted to rebuttal, he did a good job of hiding it. Instead, he sighed and redirected the conversation. He cleared his throat, "Do the police know what happened?"

"I'm not sure. They let it slip that he was some kind of famous environmentalist, but that's not much to go on."

Families with small children leisurely ambled down the street as they stretched their legs after dinner. The local eateries were pleasantly full. A few vacant tables were visible from the streets but Blue knew that would change in less than a handful of days. The arrival of the Christmas Market would bring a rush of tourists into town. Pretty soon, they'd be lucky to grab a seat at any establishment located on Heart Street.

Blue allowed her mind to wander as she enjoyed the peaceful atmosphere that felt so at odds with the information she had just shared with Charlie. Hopefully, he wasn't a blabbermouth. His astute nature and friendly eyes made it easy for Blue to trust him with an unofficial secret. A secret that was really starting to bother her.

"Maybe that information will work in your favor," Charlie drawled as he walked over to one of the more festively decorated storefronts. Cheerful garlands proudly framed the window display while a small toy train moved up and down a mountain made out of chocolate and candy canes. The chocolate store's winter display was an annual hit.

Blue grinned as she watched Charlie take in the scene. His eyes traveled across the elaborately decorated window. After a few seconds, his honey-colored orbs landed back on Blue's face. Blue moved a wayward strand of blonde hair away from her face.

"What do you mean?"

"Shoreside is a small town. I'm willing to bet that the environmentalists know each other or are at least friendly."

Excitement danced in Blue's eyes as she processed Charlie's point. She was staring her first clue in the face and hadn't even known it.

"This deserves a celebratory treat," Blue reached out and grabbed Charlie's hand. He easily followed her lead as she entered the ornately decorated confectionary.

"We're celebrating a dead body?"

Blue quickly shook her head, "No! We are celebrating our first clue. I'll start asking around town. It should be pretty easy to find at least a handful of people who know the environmentalist."

The duo stood in line behind a handful of kids tucked between their doting parents and a smattering of tween couples. Blue looked on as a few kids waved at their friends positioned throughout the winding line.

In Blue's mind, it wasn't very long ago that she had visited the chocolate store with her parents. Distant memories moved through the back of her mind like grains of sand slipping through an hourglass. Each precious moment was as fleeting as the last.

"What do you recommend?"

Blue laughed, "Anything and everything with chocolate. I have a massive sweet tooth but chocolate is my favorite."

Charlie chuckled, "I should have guessed."

"What does that mean?"

"You're very all or nothing. Not a person prone to sitting in the middle."

Blue smiled, "You learn fast. You're right, I was never one for living in the middle. I'm more comfortable living every moment in black-and-white. I guess that wouldn't apply to you."

Charlie frowned as they took another step closer to the counter. His thick brows pulled together as he tucked his chin closer to his body. Blue winced.

Her words sounded harsher than intended. Eager to explain, she added, "You're more a letter of the law instead of a spirit of the law kind of guy. I noticed how you checked the bill twice and made sure to calculate the tip to the cent. It's probably what makes you so good at your job."

"Don't flatter me. I know that I'm rigid. It's nice to have structure. I've thought about opening up my own legal practice before but it always sounded like too much risk. It's easier to have someone else deal with the risks."

A man wearing a white hat and a red apron waved in their direction. The duo stepped forward and Charlie greeted the worker.

"Hi, what would you like, Blue?" Charlie tilted his head in her direction and waited for a response.

Blue stood on the tips of her toes as she struggled to make eye contact with the worker while looking over the generously-sized ice cream cases. She projected her voice a smidge louder than necessary as she asked, "Do you still make hot fudge sundaes?"

"The best in town."

"Great. Could I please have a single chocolate scoop of ice cream and extra hot fudge?"

The man behind the counter nodded as he got started on Blue's order. He gestured to Charlie and asked, "What about you?"

Charlie chuckled, "I'll have what she's having."

"Copycat."

"The highest form of flattery."

Blue snorted, "Something like that."

The two received their treats and slowly headed out the door. A laminated flyer near the front of the store instantly captured Blue's attention. She popped the spoon into her mouth and mumbled between bites, "What do we have here?"

Chapter 7

An image of Shoreside's only lighthouse rested in the center of the flyer. Its timeless elegance looked out of place on the same page as a childish bright red squiggly font.

"For sale. Auction this weekend," Blue read the title of the flyer out loud. The paper spoon tucked inside of her cheek wobbled as she said the words out loud. How could this be true? She thought the lighthouse was on public property.

Excitement bubbled in the middle of Blue's stomach. Maybe she could buy it. She'd never be able to afford it at full price but at an auction? Maybe the odds were slowly turning in her favor. As a child, Blue spent countless hours reading beneath the shade of the towering structure. She'd drawn it hundreds of times from memory. It was a piece of Shoreside history that she wanted to lovingly claim as her own until the next generation could take over.

"Is something wrong?" Charlie leaned over Blue's shoulder as he curiously inspected the flyer. A smudge of hot fudge clung to his lower lip.

Blue pointed to the flyer and laughed, "I can't tell you how many times I've stared at this lighthouse. When I was younger, my mom and grandmother would paint the lighthouse. They would take me and we would have picnics overlooking the sea. Many of my most cherished childhood memories include the lighthouse."

Charlie chuckled, "So you are sentimental. I wasn't sure how to interpret the black and white paintings."

"Very funny. I'm an artist, of course, I'm sentimental. Besides, the lighthouse is the first thing people see after coming around the bend in the coast. It never occurred to me that it was private property. I thought it belonged to the town."

"Maybe it was recently rezoned."

A frown pulled at Blue's neatly trimmed brows. She licked her lower lip and asked, "What do you mean?"

"I usually handle zoning issues. It's possible that the town recently rezoned the land where the lighthouse is located. I'm actually here to look over a few rezoning requests."

"Now why would they do that?"

"Usually it's a great way to make money. Public land isn't very profitable so sometimes it makes more sense to sell it off."

Blue sniffed in disdain, "Not everything is about money. Sometimes you can't put a price on leaving things alone."

Charlie chuckled as he popped another spoonful of chocolate ice cream into his mouth. Chocolate smeared against the side of his lips and Blue looked away. A gentle smile inched along Blue's mouth as she handed Charlie her napkin.

"Show me where," Charlie instructed as he leaned forward and waited for Blue to point out the mess on his face. His eyes glimmered with a playful challenge that Blue was only too happy to accept. She rarely turned down a challenge. The harder things became, the more she made an effort to make sure things turned out her way.

Butterflies fluttered inside of her belly as she blotted at the sugary mess just below Charlie's lip. Blue's touch lingered a few seconds longer than necessary as she stared into two soulful eyes.

"Did you get it?"

Heat crept up the back of Blue's neck as she lowered the napkin and admitted, "Yes."

"Good. I'd hate to walk around with hot fudge and chocolate ice cream all over my face. It wouldn't be the best way to make a first impression."

"It wouldn't be the worst. You could always hit strangers with a door and then ask them on a date to keep them on their toes."

"Very funny. Do you plan on going to the auction?"

"Yeah, it wouldn't hurt to see what people want to bid for the lighthouse. I'm sure it could do with a little bit of paint. The lighthouse is the oldest structure in town."

Charlie scoffed, "Really?"

"Yep," Blue popped the p and continued, "legend has it that the first buildings were built in front of the dunes and swept out to sea."

Blue imagined drawing the scene while tucked away in her sunroom. Perhaps she'd find a little extra time in her week to create a few more paintings.

Once the remaining ice cream thawed, Blue looked over at Charlie and asked, "Would you mind walking me home?"

"I always planned on walking you back home. With a potential murderer on the loose? The tides couldn't pull me away."

A handful of stars lit the way as waves crashed along the nearby shore. Blue sucked in a deep gulp of ocean air as they trekked back to her house.

"Thank you for the date," Blue lingered near the bottom of her porch steps.

The sleek white rays of moonlight highlighted their hushed embrace on her porch. For a moment, they were the only two people in Shoreside.

"Goodnight, Blue."

Chapter 8

"Going once, going twice. Sold! Sold to the woman in the back!" The auctioneer standing in the center of the Shoreside Community Center's stage clanked his gavel and proceeded to list off the next property for sale.

Blue vaguely recognized people from several towns over as they bustled around the plastic chairs and budget concession stand. The mini muffins and burnt coffee had nothing on Melinda's shop. Blue made a mental note to get the event planner's information so she could pass it along to Melinda. Sometimes the best opportunities come from necessity.

People in the crowd were eager to bid on the cabin just outside of town. A light tap on Blue's shoulder pulled her attention away from the auctioneer shouting out numbers. Blue figured she had a few minutes before she needed to be on the lookout for her precious lighthouse. She kept telling herself that she'd only come to look, but the longer she stayed, the less that statement felt true.

"Hi, Blue! It's so good to see you. I didn't know you'd be coming to the auction. Are you bidding on anything specific? I have my eye on the old bakery just inside of town. The space would be perfect for another art gallery."

A throaty voice greeted Blue's ears. The distinct voice belonged to one of Blue's closest friends and business partners. The woman's purple hair and long white winter coat made it easy for her to stand out amongst the rest of the neutral-color-loving crowd.

"Amanda! How are you?"

"Fantastic! Your artwork keeps flying off the walls of the gallery. We might need your newest collection available sooner than expected if demand stays the same."

Amanda gave the room a cursory inspection and chuckled. The sound was honed through years of fast-paced New York parties and smoke-filled cigar rooms. She stared Blue down and arched a dyed brow. Amanda wasn't one to let her friends shy away from taking credit.

Blue modestly replied, "That's amazing news. I'm sure my family name helps with the sales."

"Everyone in a 100-mile radius knows your family. You're third-generation oil painting royalty. Don't sell yourself short, Blue. A reputation quickly built can be just as easily destroyed. Your work is exciting. You put your heart into each painting and it shows. People want your art because they speak to them."

Blue nodded as she listened to Amanda discuss the recent boom in purchases. The information only boosted Blue's resolve to consider bidding on the lighthouse. She lived frugally and kept expenses low. Perhaps she'd be able to purchase the lighthouse and restore it over time. It was no secret that the lighthouse's shingles tended to fall to the ground after the slightest winter storms. Blue wondered how many people would be willing to gamble on such a potentially tricky renovation. The most complex home improvement Blue had completed was her spare bathroom. Maybe it was time for a bigger challenge. Only if the numbers made sense, of course.

The auctioneer's voice pierced through the crowd as he announced the next property for sale. The old bakery.

Amanda heard the announcement and quickly said goodbye to Blue. Purple parted the sea of naturally-colored hair as Amanda navigated her way to the front of the auction.

The pamphlet claimed that the odder properties would be auctioned off closer to the end of the event. Blue chanced a glance at the community center's clock and inwardly groaned. The auction still had another hour left. With little to entertain herself, Blue decided to sneak in some sleuthing. It was a rare opportunity to witness so many people gathered together. Blue intended to make the most of the local gathering. Maybe one of the conversations nearby would spark some interest.

Decided, Blue ambled to the back of the room and hovered near the concession stand. She took her time as she grabbed a paper plate and selected a few painfully dry pastries. An older couple followed behind her and Blue tried her best to be invisible as she eavesdropped on their conversation. The woman groaned about how the developers in town were hogging up parking spaces along the main road. Blue topped her plate off with another muffin as she grappled to find an excuse to listen. The slim man with a left-footed lean agreed with his wife. He even moaned about the recent uptick in vacant property prices.

Blue scanned the table and realized she'd already placed one of every item onto her nearly overflowing plate. Unwilling to get caught snooping, she moved away from the concessions and sat down in one of the white plastic seats. She placed the plate on her lap and flipped through a discarded auction brochure. Sure enough, the lighthouse was proudly set to be the closing property. Did that mean they were expecting a wild bidding battle? Maybe. If people wanted the old lighthouse half as badly as Blue, then she was sure the winning bid alone would set a new record.

A group of fishermen, fresh from a morning catch, spoke a few feet away from Blue. Their annoyed grunts punctuated the conversation. One of the men rumbled, "The developers are going to poison the land and hurt the fish. I thought the wetlands were protected."

Blue sank lower in her plastic seat as she covered her face with the discarded auction pamphlet. The commotion from the crowd made it difficult to hear more than every fifth word. Blue wanted to butt into the conversation and ask for details, but she figured the group would be less inclined to speak freely with a stranger. Instead, she held still and waited until the fisherman with the deep baritone voice boomed, "It can't be a coincidence. Developers come here and suddenly all of this land is up for sale. I bet the next auction will include parts of the wetlands."

Blue narrowed her eyes as she put together the clues. What if everything was connected? She dared a careful glance around the room and realized that the fishermen could be right. Half of the people in the room weren't from Shoreside. Sure, a handful she recognized from a few towns over, but the rest? Clean and trendy coats ratted out the fast-paced city dwellers that were a far cry from the slow-moving lifestyle enjoyed in the small coastal towns.

"Last but not least, we have the famous Shoreside lighthouse!"

An excited voice rang into the air. Blue sat taller in her seat as she eagerly awaited the opening bid. She had a clear view of the auctioneer as she stared at him from a particularly empty section of the community center.

The auctioneer spoke so quickly that Blue worried she'd fall behind. What if she wasn't fast enough to place a bid? Without thinking, Blue raised her hand and hoped that the auctioneer would be able to see her. Maybe she'd have a chance to win if her bid was early enough.

"Going once, going twice. Sold!"

The auctioneer pounded the gavel and concluded the final auction for the weekend. People slowly stood from their chairs and made their way out of the room. Blue felt rooted to her seat as she tried to process what had happened. She wondered who had beaten her. The crowd murmured as she stood and proceeded to join the group.

"Wait! Miss! We need your information." A young intern with a clipboard and neatly written name tag scampered over to Blue. He reached her right as she prepared to leave.

Blue hummed, "I'm sorry to disappoint you but I don't want to join a mailing list for the auctions. I only came here for the lighthouse. But if you could give me the event's coordinator contact information that would be great. I know an awesome local coffee shop that would be great at catering this event."

She finally looked at the intern. The rest of the words prepared to zoom out of her mouth stopped right in their tracks. Blue pulled her oversized tote bag closer to her chest as she analyzed the perplexed look so clearly painted across the intern's face. Maybe he didn't know the name of the event's coordinator. Oh, well. It was worth a try.

The intern moved the clipboard into Blue's sight. He frowned, "You were the winning bid on the lighthouse."

Blue paled as she shakily accepted the clipboard and read over the information. Her mind raced a million miles a second as she searched for the price. Her eyes widened as she found the dollar amount neatly written across the bottom line.

Chapter 9

Blue blinked. As soon as her eyes refocused on the page, she still saw the same unreasonably affordable number. She looked over at the auction intern and asked, "Is that the right number?"

She made more than that in a month. A busy month like December thanks to the Christmas Market, but still. Surely this was a mistake. How could such a well-known historical property sell for so little?

Blue almost didn't have the heart to point it out. But then again, if there was a mistake it would be easier to sort it out now rather than later.

Now it was the intern's turn to appear perplexed. He double-checked the number and nodded. The intern admitted, "The lighthouse needs a few repairs. I guess most people weren't willing to put in the time and money."

Blue followed the intern to the front of the auction. She asked a few more questions before proceeding with the motions necessary to complete the auction process. Her heart threatened to pound out of her chest as she signed on the dotted line.

She didn't care if the rest of the town didn't see the vision for Shoreside's only lighthouse. With time, everything would come to light.

Chapter 10

She left the community center with a lightness to her steps. Blue couldn't wait to tell Melinda. Her cousin wasn't going to believe this. Curiosity made it difficult for Blue to focus. She could barely contain her excitement as she walked down the paved road. Blue craned her neck to the right and glimpsed the top of the lighthouse as it stood steadfast in the distance. Soon, she'd have a new project to breathe life into.

The gossip about the developers mingled at the front of her mind. Were the murmurs right? Blue figured she knew one person who might be able to unravel some of her leads. She'd need to speak with Charlie sooner rather than later. As a lawyer with zoning experience, he'd be the perfect person to answer her questions. It also felt like the perfect excuse to see him again.

With so much change, Blue tried to grasp the swiftness of the last few days. Sometimes a year's worth of events happen in the blink of an eye.

Chapter 11

"Let me get this straight, you were the only person to bid on the lighthouse?" Melinda handed Blue a steaming cappuccino as she listened to every detail about yesterday's auction. She looked over at the crowd of caffeine-hungry patrons and added, "Give me the short version of the story."

Blue laughed, "Nothing more than what I told you yesterday. I really wanted the lighthouse and my competitive nature jumped out. I still can't believe it's mine."

"Have you already seen it in person?"

"No, I'm supposed to get the keys later this week. Something about paperwork and a missing spare key."

Melinda snorted, "This waiting around might kill you."

A few murmurs from the customers behind reminded Blue to finish up the conversation. She patted the counter and pulled out her wallet. Melinda waved her off and said, "You can pay me by finishing the rest of your story once there's a break in the morning rush."

Blue laughed, "Deal."

She walked over to her usual table and pulled out one of her most recent reads. The pages were folded and bent. Blue winced, she tried to keep her books tidy but they always seemed to have a mind of their own. Her fingers leafed through the upturned pages until she finally returned to her place in the story. A contented hum left the back of her throat as she prepared to dive back into her most recent romance dime novel. She loved a happy ending.

Time moved along and soon enough Melinda settled into the opposite seat. Her short hair swept into her face as she tossed back her head and groaned, "Waiting to hear the rest of the story was torture."

Blue teased, "What makes you think there's more to the story? Isn't it interesting enough that I bought an entire lighthouse over the weekend?"

"Sure, but it's you."

"I'm not sure what that means, but I'll just take it as a compliment."

Melinda leaned forward and stole the half-eaten cookie off Blue's plate. She chewed her monstrous bite of chocolate chip cookie while Blue arched her brow, completely unfazed by her cousin's antics.

"As I was saying, the auction gave me a few more clues into the incident in the wetlands."

"You mean the dead body?"

A few heads turned in their direction and Blue kept her gaze locked on Melinda's relaxed face. She didn't want to look at the other customers and lose her nerve.

Blue sucked in another breath and simply nodded her head. "I overheard a few people talking about the developers trying to build luxury apartments. I think the developers might be tied into this but I need to find proof."

"What kind of proof?"

"Charlie said that I should focus on the environmental groups in the area. Someone will probably have more information."

Melinda smirked as she leaned back in her chair. The legs on the back of her seat squeaked against the floor as she redistributed her weight.
"Charlie, huh?"

"He's new in town. I'm helping him get acquainted with Shoreside."

"Sure you are," Melinda wiggled her brows.

Blue wadded up her unused napkin and tossed it in her cousin's direction. The two laughed when the crumpled paper ball hit the center of Melinda's forehead. Bullseye.

"Real mature."

"Aren't you the one always saying it's important to never grow up? I think it's too soon to tell. We're getting off-topic. Besides telling you about the lighthouse purchase, I also wanted to see if you're free tomorrow."

Melinda toyed with the unused napkin as she reached forward and devoured the rest of Blue's unfinished sweet treat. Melinda was about to put the remaining chunk of the cookie back on Blue's plate but Blue waved her off. If her cousin wanted the cookie, she could have it. Blue just wanted the coffee.

Between bites, Melinda murmured, "It depends on what we're doing. I just need to ask someone else to come in and watch the store."

"We need to do a little bit of outreach work. I read online that one of the local environmental groups plans to host a beach cleanup in the morning. We can go together and hopefully find more clues along the way."

"I'm in," Melinda agreed in a deadpanned voice. She playfully wiggled her brows as she asked, "Will Charlie come along?"

"I thought we could do this together. We could use one of our old tricks from high school to sneak out the information."

Melinda leaned forward and her front chair legs rattled as they pounded against the floor. She tapped the table, "Let's aim for eager newcomers. I get to be the bad cop. You can play the good cop."

"It's a beach clean up, not an interrogation." Blue tried to talk some sense into her cousin, but Melinda refused to be swayed. In the end, Blue relented and decided it would be easier to work alongside an immovable force.

"What time does the beach clean-up start?"

Blue paused as she brought out a printed invitation. Her fingers quickly scanned the paper as she searched the invite. A deflated sigh escaped, "Nine in the morning."

"On a Sunday? Now that definitely sounds like a deadly experience."

Blue laughed so hard that tears pricked the edges of her eyes. She wiped away the moisture and smiled. Excitement zinged through Blue's blood. With every passing day, she felt closer to uncovering the truth. Soon, everything would come into focus. Blue only hoped she would be able to handle the image once it came into focus.

Chapter 12

Darkness shrouded the sand dunes and left Blue feeling unusually melancholy. She reflected on the whirlwind of recent events while trudging across the damp sand. Her feet sunk down with every forward movement. In the distance, a few people gathered around a white pop-up tent.

Blue subconsciously patted her ratty old cargo pants. She wore loose-fitting clothes that she didn't mind ruining. The invite had remained vague about the expected level of exertion. Blue hoped it would be a reasonable amount of effort.

A familiar statuesque figure captured Blue's gaze. Oh, no. Melinda donned what appeared to be an outfit appropriate for a movie premiere. Her cherry red cocktail dress and shimmering ballet flats reminded Blue of a homing beacon. So much for keeping a low profile within the group. Melinda spotted Blue as she trudged across the damp sand and waved. Even from a distance, Blue heard Melinda's voice. This was going to be the longest two hours in the history of beach cleanups.

Blue waved as she joined the group. Two notably similar girls dressed in identical shirts adjusted their positions so Blue could join the informal semi-circle.

"Thanks."

The two young women nodded in unison and then returned their attention to the person closer to the center of the group. Blue was surprised at the size of the group. She casually counted the number of attendees before switching on her game face. Good cop. Bad cop.

Blue pulled back her shoulders and tried to memorize the friendly faces. A majority of the members looked like they were in college or just branching out into the professional world. Blue subtly turned from one face to the next as she attempted to commit them all to memory. Maybe the environmental group partnered with the local college a few minutes down the road. It would explain the overwhelmingly bright-eyed and bushy-tailed helpers, eagerly waiting to explore the sand.

Birds loitered near the edge of the water as they attempted to catch their early morning meals. The tide seemed to work in their favor as they dipped into the edge of the waves. Water tumbled against the shore.

The familiar sound created a soothing ambiance that helped lessen Blue's nerves. She could do this. All she needed to do was talk to a few people. A task easier said than done. How would she be able to casually bring up a dead person?

A young woman with a nose piercing walked over to Blue and smiled. "Wow! We rarely get new people. Two newcomers never happen. Do you need a baggie?"

Blue stumbled over her sentence as she repeated, "Baggie?"

The woman extended a trash bag and Blue quickly got the picture. She grinned, "Thanks. My friends call me B."

Blue stopped herself from saying her real nickname. What if word got around that someone was asking questions about the dead environmentalist? The last thing she wanted was for someone to come snooping through her very cozy and remarkably isolated lifestyle. Someone would eventually notice, but Blue didn't plan on making it easy for them.

"Nice to meet you, B. My name is Cassidy. I'm the acting president of the Coastal Campus Environmental Club. It's like really nice to see that you dressed for the occasion."

Blue shook out the trash bag as she pretended to get situated. From the corner of her eyes, she watched how Melinda strutted around the beach and pointed out small pieces of trash for other members to pick up. Blue tried her best to hide the smile that threatened to spread across her lips. Melinda was really dedicated to their good cop and bad cop routine. With one unbelievably annoying newcomer, the other person was bound to look more approachable. Blue made a mental note to thank Melinda for the seemingly unrealistic plan. It worked.

"Acting president?"

Cassidy sighed as she reached down and picked up a small shard of plastic. Blue followed along and gathered a few wayward pieces of debris as they walked near the coastline. She stuck close to Cassidy as they walked down the beach in tandem.

"Yeah. We were supposed to vote on a new president, but the professor in charge of overseeing the voting process recently passed away. It doesn't make any sense. He was a really young ecology professor."

"So, an ecology professor oversaw this group?"

Cassidy nodded, "Yeah, he was like really connected in the area. People always asked his opinions before building projects near important environmental areas. He always talked about the importance of doing the right thing for the animals. But the last few weeks he seemed distant. Always complaining about prices and money troubles, but I figured that came with the territory of being a new professor."

"I see," Blue leaned down and kept her face neutral as she waited for Cassidy to continue. After all this time, the answers were seemingly falling from a stranger's mouth. Blue did her best to remain neutral as she gained better insight into the situation.

"Do you remember anything about the night he died?"

Cassidy huffed, "Yeah, like I was really upset. We were supposed to host our holiday party and he like totally ditched. He said he needed to meet someone and left before we even cut into the cake."

Blue pushed, "Did he say who he was meeting?"

"No, but I got the feeling that it was someone important. Like a person that my professor didn't want to let down or something. You sure ask a lot of questions."

Dang it.

"Oh, it's my first time with the group. I want to get to know everyone. What's your major?" Blue pivoted the conversation and kept the rest of their talk light as they moved around the dunes. The water in the wetlands glimmered as the two stood on a particularly large sandy hill angled towards the sun.

A beeping sound rang through the air and Cassidy turned off her watch's alarm. She clapped her hands together and held up her half-filled trash bag. Her lips pressed into a thin, unimpressed line as she looked at Blue.

"Is something wrong?"

Cassidy pointed to their bags and nodded. "Yeah, we keep like collecting more trash and it really bugs me. It happens every year whenever it's almost time for the Christmas Market. The tourists visit and toss trash onto the beach. The trash ends up in the ocean and makes something that should be a really nice time something really bad for the environment."

"That's sad. I never thought about the impact tourists would have on our beaches."

Cassidy sighed, "Yeah. It's a real bummer when people don't like show enough respect for the places they visit."

Blue nodded as she looked over at the mostly filled bags other members collected. The black trash bags were a sight for sore eyes. She chanced a glance at Melinda and smirked. Her dress looked worse for wear and her trash bag was so light that it blew in the soft breeze. A few people looked annoyed as they accepted Melinda's bag and added it to their pile.

"Thanks for having me."

Cassidy shook Blue's hand. They tossed their trash bags into the pile and Blue moved to the outskirts of the group to get a better feel for the social dynamics. Clearly, Cassidy had the respect of her friends. She spoke and people listened. The group would be fine in her capable black-painted fingernails.

Blue waved goodbye and climbed her way back over the dunes. She looked over to the heart of Shoreside and noticed how the dunes stopped right after the town. The sight struck her as odd. Why would the dunes end so close to town? What if another clue was staring her right in the face and she just couldn't put it together?

Blue reached down and realized she didn't have her phone. She'd wait until she got home to call her cousin. They needed to talk.

Chapter 13

A gull cawed overheard as it landed on the rickety lighthouse roof. Blue wrinkled her nose and hoped another shingle wouldn't end up shattered. She reached into her pocket and pulled out the key to the front door.

In a few minutes, she'd see the full extent of her fixer-upper. The outside paint looked worn and drab. Blue stared at the lighthouse and frowned. What stood only a few feet in front of her was nothing like the regal structure from her memories. For some reason, it was almost as if the lighthouse had shrunk over the years. The splendor that once encased the structure now seemed lost to time. Rust crept around the metal window frames and Blue groaned. She'd bought something based on a memory and was probably about to pay the price. The past was meant to inform the future, not dictate it. Blue tried to keep the disappointment from her features as she surveyed her most expensive purchase to date.

"How did you know being annoying at the beach cleanup would work?"

Melinda laughed as she clinked her travel mug filled with coffee against Blue's. "I didn't. I thought it was the best we could get to playing good cop and bad cop. Did it work?"

"Yes. Cassidy told me a lot of helpful information. I think we could get more details from her if we tell her the truth."

Melinda shrugged as she absently toed a shattered shingle. An excited twinkle danced in her eyes as she looked up at the bird. Maybe she was hoping another shingle would fall.

"I found something interesting."

Blue snapped her head back in Melinda's direction. She narrowed her eyes. "Way to bury the lead. Tell me."

"The girls in navy striped shirts had a lot to say about the circumstances surrounding their professor's death."

"The twins?"

"Yeah, they're twins. They said the group received a threatening email just days before he died."

Blue frowned, "Did they tell the sheriff?"

"Yeah, but they didn't think the department took it seriously."

An irritated grumble left the back of Blue's throat. It always felt like concerns mentioned by women were only heeded in retrospect. Not on Blue's watch.

A flurry of questions threatened to snowball in the back of Blue's mind. Why would the best hint about the environmentalist's death be discarded? Was this untimely death slowly turning into a murder investigation? Was her gut right? She needed to see the email.

"Did you get their phone numbers?"

A slow smile inched along Melinda's face. She tilted her head to the side and teased, "Guess the bad cop in this sleuthing mission ended up with the goods after all. I got all of that while cleaning up the beach in a club dress. Imagine what I could have gotten in normal clothes."

"You're stalling."

Melinda balked, "No. I'm gloating. Look, I can text them and see if they'll send over a photo of the email. It sounded pretty suspicious."

She reached into her back pocket and swiped her fingers across her phone. Melinda put her phone away and announced, "Done."

A headache started to form in the back of Blue's head. She rubbed the side of her temple and sighed. "Everything about this is starting to feel off. What are the odds that all of this is suddenly happening at the same time?"

Melinda took a sip of her still-steaming coffee. She swished it in her mouth before she swallowed it. Blue wrinkled her nose but didn't say anything.

"You're right, Blue. This keeps getting weirder and weirder. Maybe that means we're on the right track."

"I'm starting to wish I was wrong."

Melinda snorted as she watched Blue struggle with the lighthouse's lock. She recently received the keys and couldn't wait to inspect the inside. Melinda nudged Blue out of the way with her hip. Blue relented and allowed Melinda to give it a try. Blue's hands were starting to cramp after yanking the key so roughly.

The old wooden door groaned in protest. Melinda stood back and twisted the key at the same time she bumped her hip into the frame. The door busted open and smacked the wall with a resounding *Thwack*.

"Where did you learn to do that?"

Melinda shrugged, "Sometimes the door to the coffee shop gets stuck. It needs a nudge in the right direction before it wants to open."

Blue held her breath as she stared inside. She'd imagined looking inside of the lighthouse for so long that it almost felt like a fantasy. For over 30 years, she'd stared at it from the outside. Marveling at its impressive stature and dependable glow. What if it was nothing like she'd imagined? Blue stepped forward and walked into the lighthouse. She held her breath as she looked around the dust-covered lower level. Light from the top trickled down as dust floated around in the shining rays of sunlight. Blue sneezed and rubbed her nose on the back of her sleeve. She hadn't known what to expect, but she hadn't expected so much dust. Blue tilted her head up and followed the spiral staircase as it led to two more semi-lofted levels.

Melinda's face looked tense as she split her attention between the unloved lighthouse and her cousin. She outstretched her hand and carefully returned the key to Blue's possession.

"It's perfect."

"This lighthouse is so beautiful. It's a shame so many people can't see the potential."

"Most people can only see what's right in front of them. I just wish I could see far enough into the future to know how all of this would pan out. Or well, something like that."

"See, even bad moments have pockets of good."

Blue narrowed her eyes, "Where did you read that?"

"One of my baristas wrote it down as the coffee shop's quote of the week."

"Fitting."

A dinging noise echoed off the barren walls. Blue turned to Melinda and waited. As luck would have it, one of the twins answered in less time than it took to shimmy open a stubborn door.

Melinda read the message out loud. "Stop digging or we'll bury you."

A chill raced down Blue's spine. The temperature suddenly felt several degrees colder. A tangible threat lurked within the letter. Blue licked her lower lip, "Who is it from?"

"Weird, landluver@email.com."

Blue hummed in the back of her throat as she clutched her travel mug closer to her chest. The email address was clearly a dead-end. Maybe someone made a fake email account to hide in the shadows. Or maybe, it was some weird college joke that Blue was too far removed from emerging adulthood to understand.

Melinda tucked her phone back into her pocket and sighed, "I know that look."

"What look?"

"That. That look on your face. It's the look you always get before doing something impulsive. Are you planning to buy another lighthouse?"

Blue sniffed as she intentionally looked around the empty space. Her cousin had a point. She wasn't going to let this unfolding mystery go. "We both know this lighthouse has sentimental value."

"Right. But are you emotionally attached to any other lighthouses?"

"No, but if that changes you'll be the first to know."

Melinda scrubbed her palm across her face, "I get it. You found the guy in the wetlands. You need to see this through, but what are we looking at?"

"See, that's the problem. I'm not sure. It's weird that Sheriff Lennox didn't look more closely at the emailed threat. I also don't love how the mayor seems committed to sweeping this under the rug. It's all so wrong. And don't even get me started on the developers."

"What about the developers?"

Blue placed a dainty hand on her hip as she craned her neck to look Melinda in the eyes. She huffed, "It's not a coincidence. I think the gossipy fishermen were right. The real estate auction was packed. What if the land is getting rezoned just so that they can snatch up the wetlands and build a luxury apartment complex?"

"What did Charlie say?"

Blue laughed, "I haven't told him, yet."

"No time like the present."

Chapter 14

Blue's long dress swirled around her heels as she walked down the center of Shoreside. Fittingly enough, Heart Road encompassed the majority of the small town's shops. Blue appreciated the town's sleepy unassuming beauty. Each storefront looked like a quaintly decorated coastal cottage. Muted shades of blues and pinks added a faint pop of color to the festively decorated exteriors.

Eventually, Blue stopped outside of Nico's Eatery. She looked at the time and noticed she was a few minutes early. The air felt colder than usual as it bit against Blue's rose-colored cheeks. She leaned forward and pushed against the restaurant's door.

One of the regular waiters smiled and seated her near the end of the bar. "Thank you. Can I order a hot coffee while I wait for my date?"

"Sure thing, miss."

The bubbly waiter disappeared as her high ponytail swished from one side of her shoulders to the other. Blue carefully glanced at the diners. It was an unusual time for a meal. Tuesday nights were notoriously slow but with the Christmas Market just around the corner, businesses were starting to pick up the pace. Waiters bustled around the compacted space as the conversations grew to a dull roar.

After a few sips of coffee, Blue glanced at the time and arched her brows. Charlie didn't seem like the type of person to be late, ever. Dread bubbled in the pit of Blue's stomach as she worried over potential what-ifs. Her worrying stopped short as soon as she noticed a tall figure pacing outside of the restaurant. Maybe he didn't know she was already safely tucked inside of Nico's Eatery.

Blue slapped a few dollar bills on the bar and headed over to the front door. She leaned forward and pulled with all of her weight. The door cracked open and Blue managed to hear Charlie as he spoke with someone on the phone.

"I know. The zoning is under consideration by the committee. I'll draw up a few more plans that will make it impossible to deny the development of the luxury apartments. Who wouldn't want to live right next to the beach?"

Blue blinked. She stared at Charlie as if she was just seeing him for the first time. The door to Nico's Eatery suddenly felt heavier than usual. She allowed it to close and returned to her seat at the bar. Maybe she had been too willing to overlook reason. It all made sense. Charlie worked for the developers. He was in town on a mission to turn Shoreside into a commercialized, environmental disaster. Blue tapped her fingers along the wooden bar as she contemplated her next move. A twinge of betrayal twisted her gut. She had trusted him. Had she accidentally trusted the enemy?

Her previous excitement melted away like snow on a warm summer's day. Blue's emotions simmered as betrayal twisted into anger. Charlie hadn't lied about his job, but he also hadn't told the truth. Blue told him about discovering a dead man in the wetlands and he never mentioned being part of a company determined to turn a wildlife hotspot into a concrete jungle. Blue stared at the crowd but her eyes refused to focus. How had she been so blind?

A towering figure greeted her with a warm smile. Charlie grinned, "Hi Blue. What's the big news?"

A thin smile inched along Blue's lips as she struggled to navigate the current situation. "I bought the lighthouse."

"That's amazing!" Charlie settled onto the nearest barstool and chortled. His amusement was short-lived. His grin faltered as soon as he caught wind of Blue's pensive mood. "Is something wrong?"

Blue narrowed her eyes, "I'm not sure. Why didn't you tell me that you were working for the developers?" Anger pinched her brows together as her chest heaved. Her voice sounded calmer than she felt.

Confusion momentarily covered Charlie's face as he leaned back on the stool. Understanding filled his face as he deadpanned, "You went outside to look for me and heard me talking on the phone."

"Bingo."

"Blue, I can explain. It's complicated but let me explain. I work for a development company. It's a large project and they wanted me to be in the area while they put it together."

"You don't think that's suspicious?"

Charlie tilted his head to the side as his voice took on a perplexed quality. "I don't understand why you're so upset."

Blue slid off the stool and landed on her feet. She craned her neck in Charlie's direction and huffed. Even seated on a barstool, he easily hovered over her frame. Blue regretted wearing flats as she vaguely waved in Charlie's direction and sighed, "I'm getting a headache. I need to go home."

The date crumbled to ashes before Blue's eyes. She didn't know what to think of Charlie. His phone call had thrown her for a loop. Blue had skipped around her sunroom all day while looking forward to her date. She had even planned to tell Charlie about the mysterious email. Deflated, Blue exited the restaurant as Charlie asked her to wait. It was getting dark, but Blue knew she could find her way home. She made it less than two storefronts before dark hair and gentle brown eyes entered her line of sight.

Blue sighed as Charlie hustled to catch up. Hurt shined behind his eyes. The sight made Blue internally wince. She didn't want to hurt him. Blue just needed space. After discovering a dead body less than two weeks ago, everything felt like it was moving at the speed of light. She needed some time for things to slow down before she made snap judgment errors that would come back to bite her down the road.

Charlie looked like he was about to explain. He opened his mouth and then sighed. "Did you walk or drive?"

"I walked from my house."

The two settled into an uncomfortable silence as they walked down the street. Blue mumbled, "It's just a lot. I need time to think."

"You can be mad the entire time we walk to your house. I won't even say a word. I just want to make sure you get home safe. Deal?"

Some of Blue's earlier anger dulled to a small simmer. She sucked in a deep breath and nodded her head. A small smile ghosted against her lips as she agreed.

The two walked parallel to the wetlands that sat closer inland before slowly veering towards the beach. Stars blinked in the sky as the two made the 20-minute walk in silence. Blue was grateful that Charlie kept his word. They reached her front door and locked gazes. So much was said without saying a word. Eventually, Charlie cleared his throat and took a step back.

Blue opened her front door and walked inside as an indecipherable look crossed Charlie's face. He looked at the closed door for several seconds before slowly heading back to town.

Chapter 15

Fog danced along the seemingly endless sand dunes as Blue took a long sip of coffee. A plaid shawl wrapped over her shoulders as her straw-colored hair toppled down from a bird's nest of a bun. She felt as disheveled as she looked. The calm of her morning routine acted as a soothing balm for her aching heart.

Blue spent the majority of the night thinking. After a handful of sleepless hours, she arrived at the conclusion that she needed to speak with Charlie.

She moved around her art studio and admired her latest work. A piece where several homes floated above the waves as they drifted out to sea. While it was only a rough sketch, the vision held immense promise. Blue wasn't in the mood to delve into the painting just yet. No, she had a few tasks that demanded her presence outside of her lovely home.

Blue moved through the rooms with practiced ease. She shimmied on another flowing dress and grabbed a puffy wool jacket. While the weather was unusually cold for the season, it still remained well above freezing. California coasts weren't known for their snow. Instead, weather-instigated tantrums like earthquakes and storms were more common.

Her bare feet tapped along the floor. The pink nail polish on her big toe looked a little worse for wear. Her hair? Well, Blue looked in the mirror placed directly above her front door's side table and huffed. It was best to cut her losses. The stubborn strands wanted nothing to do with the hair tie desperately attempting to keep them in order.

Blue opened the door and paused. A pink wooden stool and a can of pepper spray rested in the center of her front porch. She didn't need to check the note hastily taped to the side of the stool to know who the gifts were from. Blue admired the small lighthouse carved into one of the stool's back legs. The little detail looked too similar to Shoreside's rickety old lighthouse to be a coincidence.

"He knows how to carve wood?" Blue raised a single brow as her fingers carefully ghosted above the intricate design. A mixture of feelings swirled within Blue's belly as she carefully placed the stool inside of her house. She latched the small pepper spray onto her keychain and headed on her way.

Decided, Blue stuffed her toes into a pair of white sneakers and headed into town. In her rush, Blue forgot to lock the door. The habit wasn't ingrained into her limbs since she'd only started using the front latch less than two weeks ago. The wooden stool and small pepper spray were a lot to ask for, but Blue was willing to try. Not all change was welcomed with open arms. She headed into town with the sun against her back and the fog lapping along her feet.

Chapter 16

"Gee, what made you so Blue?"

The line always brought a flicker of a smile to Blue's face. She covered her face with her palms and groaned, "I think I ruined everything with Charlie."

Melinda looked at the ever-growing line of customers waiting for coffee before she flicked a glance at her deflated cousin. Without hesitating, Melinda rounded the counter and announced, "Taking a small break!"

Two people behind the counter groaned as Melinda plopped down at the first available table. She caught Blue's inquisitive stare and explained, "Perks of owning the joint. Besides, what are cousins for?"

Blue nodded and sank down into the seat. The familiar scenery helped loosen Blue's tongue as she struggled with where to start.

As if reading her mind, Melinda suggested, "How about starting from the beginning?"

"We agreed to go on another date. I saw him talking on the phone outside of

Nico's Eatery. I pushed open the door and heard him talking to his boss. He works for the development company. Charlie's working to rezone the wetlands so that the land can be used for the luxury apartments."

"Yikes," Melinda nodded her head and encouraged her cousin to continue.

"Understatement of the year. I was about to tell him about what we learned from the environmental group. But."

Blue stopped and huffed as she tried to put what she was feeling into words. The last few weeks were like a whirlwind of highs and lows. She took a moment to organize the full picture before she continued, "But I felt betrayed. A small part of me was afraid that he didn't want to tell me because he had something to do with the environmentalist's death. In retrospect, that sounds silly. Why would Charlie work so hard to help me investigate a murder if he was the murderer? I don't know."

The crowd experienced a lull as people went outside with their coffees to enjoy the day. With a handful of days before the Christmas Market, the town was practically overrun with tourists. Melinda's coffee shop was booming.

"I think you know and that's the problem."

Blue frowned, "What do you mean?"

"Charlie is the first man you've told me about in years. Heck, have you even dated since college?"

"Shut up. There were endeavors."

Melinda rolled her eyes at her cousin. She pushed, "See! He's something different and different can be scary. To be fair, his job does make him sound like a stuffy city brownnose."

Blue quickly added, "There's more."

"More?"

"He left a stool and a keychain-sized pepper spray on my front porch."

Melinda hummed, "I guess you have your answer."

"I guess I'll just wing it."

Riotous laughter bounced off the shop walls. Melinda sucked in a breath and brayed like a donkey. She laughed so heartily that tears threatened to fall from her eyes.

"What's so funny?"

"You haven't winged things in years. You used to be so free-spirited and connected to your intuition. You've been more yourself these past few weeks than you have in years. Your spark is back."

A newfound sense of levity hummed in Blue's chest as she took Melinda's advice to heart. She reached out and squeezed Melinda's hand. "Thanks, M. I'll go look for Charlie."

"Don't thank me, yet."

Chapter 17

For a newcomer in Shoreside, Charlie sure knew how to hide like a professional. Blue spent over two hours going up and down the street, searching for him. Blue waved each time she passed Melinda's coffee shop. By the third round, Blue decided to walk on the opposite side of the street. She had his phone number, but something about speaking in person just sounded better. Her gut said it needed to be face-to-face. So here she was, wandering around the heart of Shoreside like a sightseeing tourist.

Blue wiped a bit of sweat away from her brow and sighed. Maybe she'd run into Charlie later. It would happen in its own time. Hopefully sooner rather than later.

Bright windows lined with Christmas lights entered Blue's field of vision. A purple head bobbed around the art-filled room as tourists admired the remaining pieces. Blue pushed open the art gallery's door and smiled. She instantly noticed several missing pieces. The art was selling like hot chocolate on a cold winter's day. Amanda excused herself from talking to a young couple and made a beeline for Blue.

Amanda nodded her head in the direction of Blue's remaining pieces and teased, "See what I mean?"

"You weren't kidding." Blue eyed the lofted art gallery and smiled. Her mother and grandmother had their pieces proudly displayed inside of the proudly displayed private collection titled the Wickam Witches. Blue didn't love the title, but she understood its relevance when it came to her family's history. The upper gallery pieces provided insight into Shoreside's artistic lineage and weren't for sale. Not that that stopped the occasional plucky tourist. It always filled Blue with mirth whenever Amanda told her about customers interested in buying her family's work. Some things were just too precious to part with, but that didn't mean that they couldn't be shared with the world. At least, that's how Blue felt about her family's artwork. Too precious to be sold and too important to be hidden away. Displaying them in the art gallery felt like the perfect compromise.

Blue stared at her grandmother's interpretation of the shoreline and frowned. Had those dunes and lines in the sand always been there? She sent Amanda a curious look and asked, "Do you see that painting my grandma did of the town?"

Amanda leaned back and followed Blue's extended finger. Amanda nodded, "Yeah. People always tell me to sell it, but I always say it's part of the private collection."

"Thank you, Amanda. Do you see the way she drew the sand? It looks taller than what I paint."

"I'm not sure I understand what you're saying, Blue."

Amanda tapped her fur-lined loafers against the pristine marble floor as she tried to follow Blue's train of thought. Maybe it was just a creative difference that Blue had never realized until now. Her gut knew it wasn't a creative difference. Something else was going on. Blue's grandma had spent hours teaching her about the importance of accurately painting the world. It didn't make sense for her grandma to spend so much time emphasizing accuracy only to change her mind when it came to her own works. One thing was certain, the previous version of the shoreline was nothing like the current one. Blue suddenly felt an itch to get to the bottom of her newest family-related mystery.

"It was good to see you, Amanda."

Blue hugged her friend and headed out the front door. A throaty voice hollered just as the front door closed, "Don't forget to bring more paintings."

"On the list," Blue pulled out her phone and huffed. Her battery was dead. Maybe now was the perfect time to take her investigation old school. Blue walked down Heart Street and headed in the direction of the local library.

Chapter 18

"How can I help you, Dearie?" A kind weathered face poked out from behind a freestanding bookcase. She pushed her glasses up the bridge of her nose and headed in Blue's direction.

"Hi. Do you know if the library has any records related to the shoreline? I'm an artist and I've noticed a difference between how my grandmother drew the coastline and how I draw the coastline."

Excitement sparkled in the librarian's time-aged eyes as she took in Blue's appearance. "You're a Wickam! I was friends with your grandmother. We went to high school together. Come with me, Dearie."

Blue followed behind the older woman and she effortlessly weaved between the packed bookshelves. It was nice to hear from someone that knew her grandmother. Time had an odd way of ebbing and flowing. Some days it felt like her mother and grandmother were ages away and others it felt like they had never left. Blue didn't like to talk about the car accident that had simultaneously claimed both matriarchs.

Time healed the wound but it still left a scar along her heart.

"Blue?"

Blue realized she stopped between bookcases. She coughed out an apology and quickly scrambled to catch up with the spry librarian. They twisted and turned around the stacks until finally reaching a restricted section.

The librarian turned to Blue as a mischievous glint entered her gaze. "I never get to use this key. No one ever asks to see Shoreside's history."

Blue watched as the librarian unlocked the restricted bookshelf and wandered away. She took a step back and leisurely read over the spines. Some books detailed the history of Shoreside and others explored Shoreside's chocolate making history. A bubble of laughter escaped Blue's throat. Maybe she'd read the chocolate book after all of the mysteries were solved. Near the end of the bottom shelf, Blue found a spine that caught her eye. She knelt down and read one of the book titles out loud, "The topography of Shoreside's beaches 1800 to 1950."

Close enough.

She leafed over the pages and started to add color into her once black-and-white picture of her town. Blue quickly realized a pattern, the dunes were prone to erosion whenever the town expanded into the wetlands. She guessed the heavier foot traffic across the dunes closest to the town didn't help.

"Dunes are dynamic," Blue mulled over the sentence out loud.

After a few more hours, Blue realized her grandmother was right. She had painted Shoreside as it was. Blue was painting Shoreside as it currently stood. Inspired, she walked over to the librarian and thanked her for the help. Blue left the library and headed straight for her home. She had a feeling that the final clues necessary to start piecing this mystery together were safely tucked inside of her art studio.

Chapter 19

The wind spun grains of sand into the air. Blue spluttered as her hair pressed against her face. She was a few minutes away from her home. Soon, she'd be safely nestled inside of her art studio which lovingly doubled as an impressive sunroom. Not that there was much sun to speak of. Darkness loomed on the horizon even though it was only noon. Even the waves sounded angrier than usual as they pounded against the shoreline. Maybe Blue's mood was worse than she thought. How could waves sound angry?

Blue sped into her home and froze. She hadn't locked the door. The pink stool and pepper spray positioned only a few feet away from the poorly protected door felt ironic.

"Next time," Blue closed her door and checked the bottom lock. Satisfied, she pulled out her phone and tried to call Melinda.

"It's dead." Blue huffed and tossed her dead phone next to her paintbrushes. She looked around her sunroom and smiled.

The art brightened the room. She glanced at a vase her mother had painstakingly created and grinned. The Wickams were a famously creative family. Maybe after losing her grandmother and mom, Blue had become afraid of taking creative risks. She'd accidentally adhered to an artistic rhythm that no longer served her. "Maybe Melinda was right. I need to follow my intuition."

Her newest creation rested against an easel. Blue narrowed her eyes as she stared at the painted sky. The chaos from the day melted away as she focused on creating something beautiful. What would happen if she added a dot of color? Her fingers moved on instinct as she pulled out yellow and gold paint. She mixed the two colors together on a new palette and envisioned the night sky. Blue closed her eyes and recalled the brilliance of the stars when Charlie walked her home. Her fingers worked the paints together until the appropriate color slowly came to life. Satisfied, she dabbed and stroked the brilliant color into the previously darkened sky.

After a few hours, Blue wiped her hands on a spare towel and took a few steps back. A pleased grin inched along her lips once she noticed how nicely the pop of color complimented her work. The idea for her newest collection was slowly coming together.

Blue moved around the room and inspected three generations of Wickams. Her grandmother's shoreline made two things clear. The sparse collection of buildings was set back from the water. They had adhered to the legend and avoided interfering with the majority of the coastal wetlands. In contrast, Blue's mother's paintings spoke of a more expanded town. The dunes were lower and a bit of the wetlands visible in her grandmother's previous work had been turned into a row of track cottages.

"The wetlands protect the shore," Blue recognized the pattern. She finally understood why Shoreside's lower streets tended to flood. The streets were built over part of the wetlands. Without a natural barrier, increased flooding felt inevitable.

A smirk inched along Blue's lips. She would bring her findings to the mayor. Rezoning the wetlands would spell disaster for the town. Pride filled Blue's chest. She'd been staring at a clue all along.

Blue moved between three generations of art as a surge of pride filled her bones. She knew where she came from. The scenic pictures told the literal origins of her home while her own artwork detailed the ever-flowing present. Now, she just needed to know what was likely to happen in the future. Time always had a way of pushing people in the right direction; if only they were willing to listen.

She stood back and realized how dark the sky looked. Clouds swirled above the sea and sent alarm bells ringing in the back of Blue's mind. She padded over to her phone and realized it was still dead. Blue plugged her phone in and waited until the screen came to life.

Oh, no.

The message indicator kept going up. How long had she gone without a phone this time? Her phone beeped as a long stream of missed messages landed in her inbox.

A knock sounded at her front door. The hairs on the back of Blue's neck stood on end as she cautiously moved away from her phone. Who could that be?

Chapter 20

Blue brought the pink stool over to her front door. She mentally thanked Charlie for the gift as she looked outside. Melinda impatiently stood outside as she paced from one end of the porch to the other.

"Open the door! If you've been murdered then I'm going to haunt you in the next life!"

Blue rolled her eyes as she nudged away the stool and opened her door. "I'm pretty sure that's not how that works. If I'm murdered then wouldn't that mean I end up haunting you?"

Melinda sped over from the opposite end of the porch and embraced Blue in a crushing hug. Her cousin pressed her face into her shoulder and blubbered a few indiscernible sentences. Blue wrapped her arms around Melinda and waited for her to calm down.

Eventually, Melinda pulled far enough away from Blue's shoulder for her blubbering to turn back into words. "And that's why I need your help."

Blue frowned, "Can you say that again?"

"Haven't you been watching the news?"

"No, my phone died and I spent the day working on a few things."

Melinda grumbled, "You pick the worst day of the year to go fully off the grid."

Blue's lips pulled together as she led Melinda into the kitchen. She turned on the kettle and waited for the water to boil. "What's wrong? Melinda, you're scaring me."

Fear coiled in Blue's belly. Had another body been found? Was it someone from the environmental event? Horrible thoughts whirled around in the back of Blue's mind like an impressive hurricane.

"We're having a storm."

Blue leaned against her white kitchen counter and arched a skeptical brow. "You never worry. Why are you panicking over a storm? You love walking home after work in the rain."

Melinda sucked in a breath, "They say it's going to be the worst storm of the century. It'll reach Shoreside in less than 24 hours."

The kettle hissed as the water reached a boiling point. Blue and Melinda

stood together in silence as they pondered
their next move.

Chapter 21

Blue hefted another sandbag into her arms as she walked behind Melinda. The roughened fibers scratched against her forearms as she added another bag to the growing row blocking off the front of Melinda's coffee shop. The pile was already to Blue's waist. Not that that information was saying much.

"Thanks for helping me, Blue."

"You're my cousin. It's what we do. Besides, I could use a workout," Blue wheezed as she plopped another sandbag onto the pile. Sweat trickled down her neck and dampened the collar of her t-shirt.

"Yeah, I still don't know what to expect from something called the storm of the century." Melinda placed another wooden board across the storefront windows and hammered away.

"Lucky us," Blue lifted another sandbag and then patted the pile. She slid down to the floor and cupped her chin in the palm of her hands. Her heart felt like it was about to beat out of her chest. The sandbags were heavier than they looked.

"Have you spoken to Charlie?"

Blue frowned as she stuck out her lower lip and groaned, "No. I left my phone at home. I wanted to help you with the store as quickly as possible. Guess I left it on the counter."

"I'm starting to think you hate technology," Melinda climbed down the ladder and inspected her handiwork. It looked sturdy enough. Besides, Heart Street was safely tucked behind the dunes. The only street built over the wetlands was recently sold off in parts at the recent real estate auction.

"No, it's just easier to take life slowly."

"Right, but this storm isn't going to wait five to six business days for you."

Blue leaned back against the sandbags and sighed, "You're right."

She observed as other local business owners also spent the afternoon boarding up their beloved shops. Blue watched as an odd mix of locals and tourists bustled through the street. For once, people weren't lingering. The clouds overhead looked even more ominous than before.

"What time did the news say the storm would arrive?"

"Later tonight. I think sometime after nine? In true reporter fashion, I'd give that number some grace."

Disappointment covered Blue's features as she mumbled, "The storm will destroy any remaining evidence left in the wetlands. We'll have nothing to work with."

"Not true. You'll just need to get creative. Traces of the truth always linger."

Blue nodded as she leaned against the sandbags and hauled herself back onto her feet. She had a feeling her home would be fine. It was the only building in Shoreside protected by both the wetlands and the sand dunes. She was suddenly grateful that her walks into town felt so long. The more distance, the better.

"I should probably start heading home." Blue paused and looked over at Melinda's leftover supplies. An image of the lighthouse popped into the back of her mind. She pointed to a few tarps and asked, "Can I have your leftover supplies?"

Melinda waved her hands at the pile and laughed, "All yours."

Chapter 22

Raindrops landed on Blue's waterproof jacket as she shoved the last of the supplies into the lighthouse. Melinda had asked Blue if she needed help, but Blue had easily waved her off. Melinda needed to keep an eye on her store. The coffee shop was Melinda's main source of income and Blue's favorite place in town to grab a tasty treat.

Blue rammed her shoulder against the heavy wooden door and groaned. It looked so much easier when Melinda did it. She flicked on her battery-powered lantern and inspected her supplies. She grabbed a few tarps and figured she could use them to cover the roof. If she wasn't careful, flying shingles were about to be the least of her concerns.

Shadows yawned across the curved walls as Blue carefully ascended the winding staircase. The metal railing shook with her weight but remained surprisingly strong. Blue peaked at the second floor before she proceeded to the third. Darkness skittered away as Blue raised the intensity level on the lantern. The added boost illuminated the darker corners and helped Blue see what she considered to be the best part of the lighthouse. She left the steps and pushed against the small wooden door. It opened without much fuss and revealed the lantern room. Blue gasped as she took in the sight. She stood at the very top of the lighthouse and moved closer to the glass. Blue looked out one of the windows and admired the cottages dotted along the shore. Lights shone from a handful of homes and beat back the darkness.

For the first time, Blue witnessed Shoreside in all of its beauty. The image felt permanently ingrained in Blue's heart. She thought about crafting a black and white painting to capture the scene but it didn't feel right. The sight wasn't something that could be brought to light without using a bit of color. The clarity she once found in her black-and-white life melted away as she embraced the vibrancy of color. The uncertainty seemed to make moments even sweeter. She mentally promised to paint the view using as many colors as necessary.

Commotion from below grabbed Blue's attention. A figure moved around the outskirts of the lighthouse. Blue squinted but the person's face was shrouded in darkness.

It could be anyone. Fear pulsed through Blue's veins as she watched the stranger press against the lighthouse's front door. The door she'd forgotten to lock behind her after carrying in all of the supplies. A boom resounded around the lower level of the lighthouse as Blue sucked in a deep breath. She was no longer alone.

Chapter 23

"Blue!" A deep voice boomed from below. The tension deflated from Blue's shoulders like air from a balloon on a hot summer's day. She absently clutched the keychain mace in her left hand while the other handled the lantern.

She left the lantern room and cautiously maneuvered the stairs. Blue called down, "Charlie?"

A faint light danced around the lower level of the lighthouse. Blue recognized the outline of Charlie's figure as he stood a few paces away from the front door.

"What are you doing here?"

Charlie scoffed, "I was worried about you." His gaze traveled down to the keychain mace still clutched in Blue's hand. A small smirk inched along his lips but he didn't comment on the sight. Smart man.

Blue stopped a few inches away from Charlie's drenched form. She looked around the sparse room and handed him a towel. "Why were you worried?"

"How could I not be? You recently found a dead body. There's a storm of the century only hours away from reaching land. My phone calls kept going to your voicemail and Melinda flagged me down this afternoon and said you were looking for me."

"Okay, I see your point. I'm sorry about the phone. It died and I've never been great about checking it. Here, take another towel."

"Thanks. What are you doing at the lighthouse instead of your home?"

Blue winced, "I wanted to toss a tarp onto the roof. The shingles keep flying off. I don't even want to imagine what will happen to the roof once a massive storm arrives."

Charlie shook out his hair and grunted as he rolled up his sleeves. He looked over at Blue as he collected the tarp and mumbled, "Lead the way."

The roof never looked better. Well, it never looked so well protected. Thick tarps were tied and weighted down across the surface. Blue watched as Charlie closed one of the windows in the lantern room and announced, "Done."

Blue checked him over as remorse filled her chest, "You're soaked. In this place, you might catch a cold."

"I'll dry off," Charlie removed his hoodie and gratefully accepted the towels he had refused earlier. Blue averted her eyes as Charlie removed his shirt. The cotton material clung to his chest as he pulled it over his head. Blue snuck a glance before she physically turned her body in the opposite direction.

A throaty chuckle invaded the tight space. Charlie spoke with a smile in his voice, "You can look, Blue. We can't ignore each other for the duration of the storm."

Blue turned around just as Charlie's dampened features came into view. Lightning struck the sea and momentarily illuminated the room. Water dripped from his strong jaw and fell to the floor. The pink and gold beach towels slung over his shoulders only added to his siren appearance. Heat traveled to Blue's cheeks as she blushed.

Another bolt of lightning hit the sea. Blue's jaw slackened with a sudden realization. They were stuck inside for the evening. She stared into Charlie's eyes. The temperature within the unheated lighthouse managed to creep up several degrees as the two entered an informal staring battle.

Blue cleared her throat and looked down as she tried to collect her thoughts. "You came looking for me." Her voice was so quiet that part of her expected her words to get gobbled up by the storm.

"You called. Not literally, it seems your phone skills are a little rusty."

Laughter filled the small space as Blue rubbed her palms together. The earlier electricity between their bodies lessened to a light current. It felt nice to be able to talk to someone so easily. Blue ran a hand through her disheveled hair and sighed, "I'll work on it. In my defense, it rarely ever rings. The last few weeks have been unusual."

A shiver raced down Blue's back as she met Charlie's observant stare. He opened one of the towels and gestured for her to approach.

Blue shook her head, "You'll freeze."

"We can share. It's a pretty large blanket. Don't tell me you're more afraid of cooties than freezing to death."

"Cooties?"

Charlie chuckled as Blue closed the distance and nestled into the warm fabric. She wrinkled her nose, "I haven't heard that word in forever."

"I haven't said that word in forever." Charlie rubbed the top of Blue's shoulders. The friction helped to ward off some of the earlier chill. Not for the first time, Blue was glad that she only needed to fend off an unpleasant West Coast winter. An East Coast winter with only two beach towels to keep warm? Not a chance.

The silence felt peaceful as they sat together and stared out the windows. They stared into the distant stormy sky as the wind howled around the lighthouse. Blue looked at the light positioned in the center of the room and narrowed her eyes. What if she could turn it on? She searched around and found a relatively large switch positioned near the corner of the room. Blue turned to Charlie as an excited sparkle danced in her eyes. "If this switch turns on the light then I'll tell you what I found out from a local environmental club."

"If it doesn't turn on?"

Blue tilted her head as a small smile inched along her lips. She flipped the switch and the light illuminated the room. Blue blinked as she stared at Charlie. She teasingly wiggled her brows and explained, "I was going to tell you, either way."

Charlie's features contorted with uncertainty. "I thought you didn't trust me."

"I just didn't know how to organize the entire picture. I was looking at it too closely. It was easier after taking a step back."

"What did you see after taking a step back?"

Blue shrugged one of her shoulders as she approached. "I saw that it didn't make sense for you to help me if you were involved with the environmentalist's death. I don't think you'd walk a mile in the rain to check on me if your intentions weren't true." Blue paused before she added, "Thank you for the gifts."

Charlie smirked, "I'm glad you thought to use the mace."

"I'm glad I didn't use it."

"Me too."

They both burst into laughter as the lightbulb in the center of the lantern room radiated a profound glow. It allowed Blue to see the faint smile lines drawn into the sides of Charlie's cheeks. A dimple appeared every time he grinned wide enough for Blue to see his teeth. Calm settled over the room as Charlie helped Blue get arranged inside of the pile of extra large beach towels.

"I'm sorry for not telling you about my job, Blue. I didn't want you to think I was tied to this mess. I was afraid about what you'd think of me and somehow managed to make everything worse. I want to make things right."

Blue placed her hand over the top of Charlie's. She nodded her head, "Thank you. I realize that now. While we were outside of the restaurant, it was a lot to process. I missed talking to you these last few days. I found a few more clues and I didn't know who else to tell. Besides Melinda, of course."

Charlie's face softened. He coughed as emotion clung to the back of his throat. "What kind of clues?"

Blue shook out her shoulders as she pointed towards the dunes that were heavily shrouded by rainfall. "It was right in front of me. I have three generations of coastal paintings sitting in my sunroom and I finally figured it out. The wetlands act as a barrier. The town was mostly built behind the wetlands. Over the years, the dunes have moved. The area where the wetlands were removed to build houses has very few dunes. I'm willing to bet the street built over the old part of the wetlands will flood. I don't want to be right, but my gut says my home and all of the other buildings built behind the wetlands will be fine."

Charlie nodded, "Maybe we can find some old photos of the coastline to back up your theory. When done right, zoning takes topography into consideration."

A pleased smile inched across Blue's lips as she teased, "So I'm right."

Charlie laughed, "Yes, you're right. Let's get more data to prove it. I've also started paying more attention to what's happening in the company. The Vice President of Finance has an odd relationship with our CEO."

Blue frowned as she tilted her head to the side, "What does that mean?"

"He just seems angry every time the CEO speaks at a meeting. I'll try to follow the CEO around, which shouldn't be too hard since we work pretty closely."

The storm outside picked up in ferocity. The wind pelted the lantern room's window with golf ball-sized water droplets. Blue felt grateful to be in such a well-positioned structure. The awkward rocky hill placed them out of harm's way. Blue hoped the same was true for the rest of Shoreside.

"I have to tell you what I found."

Charlie chuckled, "How did I know you'd manage to find something?"

"Well, don't just thank me. Melinda helped. She took on a very interesting interpretation of the good cop and bad cop routine."

Charlie furrowed his brows as his soulful eyes looked at Blue for an explanation. Blue waved a hand in the air and explained, "Before you ask, no we didn't impersonate police officers. We went to one of the local beach cleanup events at the beach. Apparently, the body I found in the wetlands belonged to a professor. The students told us about a very strange email that the club received   just days before he died."

"What was the message?"

Blue hummed in the back of her throat as she tried to recall the message word-for-word. "Stop digging or we'll bury you."

Silence passed between them as Charlie processed the new piece of information. His brows pressed together with concern as his gaze traveled to something in the distance that Blue couldn't see. Maybe he was thinking about something related to the clue.

Blue added, "The email address sounded like a dead end."

"What was it?"

Blue shrugged her shoulders as she picked at a loose strand. She sighed, "Something like land lover."

The words seemed to electrify Charlie's form. He sat a little taller as he sucked in a deep breath. "Are you sure?"

Charlie seemed torn. After a pause, he admitted, "I've seen an email like that."

"Where?"

"That's the email address the CEO uses on his to-go food deliveries."

Excitement bubbled in Blue's belly. She looked outside and groaned. They needed to wait for the storm to pass before investigating the clue.

"Are you sure?"

Charlie chuckled, "I remember it because it sounded so lame. Maybe he's a little overconfident in his ability to get away with murder."

"We don't know that for sure."

Charlie nodded, "Not yet."

Chapter 24

Blue leaned against the side of Charlie's shoulder as they waited for the storm to pass. A light sprinkling of rain pelted against the windows. The once-darkened sky glimmered with the faintest promise of a new day.

They'd spent the night talking in the lighthouse's lantern room. Blue rubbed the corners of her eyes as she ignored sleep's call. It felt nice to feel so safe.

She looked at the light in the center of the room as it performed its outdated job of warning sailors away from the unexpected curve in the shore. "It's beautiful."

"Breathtaking." Charlie's gaze landed on the side of Blue's face. They sat for a few more hours before the rain changed to a faint mist. Blue looked over to the opposite corner of the room and giggled. Charlie's sweater and shirt were still drenched. As if to strengthen the observation, a few droplets of water fell from the clothes and pooled on the wooden floor.

Charlie stretched his legs as he noticed the improving weather. His voice sounded rough as he yawned. "I think I have an idea."

"Yeah, maybe we can sprint without getting too wet."

Charlie chuckled, "No. I have an idea about solving the murder."

Blue's eyes twinkled with curiosity, "Oh?"

"I'll arrange a lunch meeting with my company's CEO. I'll get him to order the food using his email address. I might be able to get more information out of him by bluffing."

"That sounds dangerous."

"More dangerous than murder?"

Blue groaned, "I don't know. This feels like kicking the hornet's nest."

"We're running out of time. The wetlands are in the process of being rezoned. If the land's rezoned then the wetlands will go up for sale at the next real estate auction. Aren't the auctions a monthly occurrence?"

Blue brought her gaze back down to the pesky thread that kept coming loose near the edge of the blanket. "I wish we had another way to link together the culprit. An email is pretty shaky evidence."

"Right, that's why I can pretend to know more. Push a little to see what he shares."

Blue tapped her fingers along the frayed corner of the towel as her mind danced over a few alternative options. "What if it's not your CEO?"

"The evidence doesn't look good."

"Right, but what if someone used his email to send that message? Or what if he's not working alone? What if it was Cassidy from the Coastal Campus Environmental Club?"

"Who?"

"Cassidy is now the president or interim leader of the club since her professor's death."

Charlie teased, "I don't think it makes sense to kill someone over an extracurricular position."

"I know, but it's still a motive. Technically, she now has a better position in the club."

"Fine, I respect that you're being thorough."

Blue closed her eyes and thought back to her odd interactions with Sheriff Lennox. She grumbled, "What if Sheriff

Lennox is involved? He still hasn't called me back or asked me any more questions."

"I guess we'll just need to get creative when it comes to investigating. We've collected enough clues to start looking in the right direction."

"Luckily, creativity is my specialty."

Blue smiled as the first rays of morning sunlight crept along the horizon. Storm clouds moved into the distance as a relieved sigh escaped her lungs. She untangled her limbs from the towels and walked over to the windows. The windows were low enough that Blue didn't need to stand on the tips of her toes to get a good view. In the distance, Blue noticed how the dunes were rearranged. The wetlands looked fuller than usual. It was obvious some of the ocean's higher waves had traveled the distance of the sand and mingled with the freshwater.

She looked at the cluster of buildings in the distance and sighed. Heart Street looked relatively unscathed. The same couldn't be said for the recently abandoned street built over a portion of the wetlands. Blue placed a hand over her heart as she inspected the damage. Debris covered the shattered windows while once-proud porches toppled into the ground.

"We have to tell the mayor. The wetlands can't be rezoned. Do you see that lower street?"

Charlie stood and ambled over to Blue. The heat of his body invaded her senses and made it hard for her to stay on topic. She pointed to the decimated lower street and continued, "We need to keep the wetlands. The luxury apartments will get flooded if they're built on the wetlands and the animals will have nowhere to go."

Charlie mulled over Blue's words and nodded. "We might be able to get through to the town by asking them who stands to benefit the most from the apartments."

"What do you mean?"

"I think the mayor isn't telling the truth."

Blue paused as she mulled over Charlie's suggestion. Suddenly the mayor's request to hide the environmentalist's death from the public made sense. He wasn't trying to avoid scaring off tourists before the Christmas Market, he was trying to avoid attracting more attention to his nefarious activity.

"He definitely has a better motive than Cassidy from the Coastal Campus Environmental Club."

Charlie chuckled, "Now we just need to prove it."

Blue rubbed her hands together as the tendrils of a plan started to weave together in the back of her mind. She tilted her head up as she stared into Charlie's eyes and asked, "Are you thinking what I'm thinking?"

"Let's set a trap."

Chapter 25

Melinda muttered as she scrubbed down a table and moved to a wayward chair. Blue helped put away the freshly cleaned dishes as the coffee shop wound down for the night.

As expected, the coffee shop was unscathed. Blue almost regretted putting up the sandbags. Almost.

The two still needed to take down the last few boards covering up the windows. After a chaotic first morning back, Melinda still looked great. She kept pace with Blue as they swiftly closed down the shop.

"I still think this is a bad idea. Trust me, if I think something is a bad idea then it's probably a horrible idea."

Blue huffed as she bent down and grabbed the last large coffee mug from the back of the dishwasher. With her head still shoved into the back of the appliance, she retorted, "See! That's how I feel! Charlie said that he would be careful but that doesn't make me feel any better."

Melinda finished cleaning the final table. She tossed the cleaning products into the cabinet. Her voice held a concerned quality as she contemplated, "I wish we had a magic insurance policy to make sure everything goes alright."

Blue poked her head over the counter and asked, "What did you say?"

"I wish you had an insurance policy."

"Maybe we do. I think it's time I pay Sheriff Lennox another visit."

Melinda nodded as she locked the supply closet. "Make sure to bring him a gift. I'm pretty sure he just celebrated 20 years on the force."

"How does everyone keep track of that?"

"Small town."

Chapter 26

Blue held a small cactus in one hand as she raised her fist and politely knocked on the door. Her phone awkwardly dug into her hip as it moved around in the front pocket of her jeans. She knew Charlie hadn't loved the idea, but he'd begrudgingly agreed to loop in the sheriff. It was a compromise that would help Blue feel better.

Before she could knock a second time, Linsy pulled it wide open. She smiled and quickly ushered Blue inside.

"Come inside! So good to see you again, Blue. Is everything okay?"

Blue licked her lower lip and took a moment to really look at Linsy. She was sweet and thoughtful. Blue knew that Linsy and Lennox shared a unique professional relationship that mirrored a tightly-knit family. Unlike the mayor, Sheriff Lennox had never given her a reason to feel wary. Decided, Blue stepped into the small office and settled into one of the chairs. To her surprise, it creaked beneath her weight.

Linsy frowned, "I'm sorry. We need to get new chairs, but Sheriff Lennox refuses to ask for more money. The mayor keeps tightening the budget and Sheriff Lennox keeps tightening his lips. Stubborn man." Linsy's tone took on a remarkably sour tone as she spoke about the financial slight.

Bingo.

Blue weighed her options and decided it was a risk worth taking. Her gut said Linsy and Sheriff Lennox could be trusted.

"Is Sheriff Lennox in? I need to speak with him. It's about the body."

Linsy leaned closer and whispered, "Sheriff Lennox will be back from his lunch in a few more minutes. He loves grabbing a turkey sandwich from Nico's Eatery." Linsy paused and looked around the room. The action felt almost comical given the confined space. Still, the older woman checked her surroundings before she continued, "He said you found Professor Matt. His students spoke fairly about him."

Blue nodded as she realized it was the first time that she'd ever heard the professor's real name. The entire situation felt so strange. It felt like Blue was walking a tightrope as she struggled to choose her words. She wanted to speak with Linsy before Sheriff Lennox returned from his break.

"Do you know if it was an accident?"

A simple question with big implications. Blue watched as different emotions clearly moved across Linsy's face. The one that stuck out to Blue told her everything she needed to know.

"I can't tell you that, Blue. Sheriff Lennox should be here soon and maybe he'll be able to help. Is everything alright?"

Linsy was known as a warm and clever woman. She also had a reputation for having a backbone made from stronger stuff. It made sense why she and Sheriff Lennox worked so well together.

"I don't know, Linsy. I have a hunch. Well, at this point it's more than a hunch."

Sheriff Lennox strode into the room with a paper bag and a drink holder in tow. He looked over at Linsy and announced, "I brought you a tuna sandwich. Told Nico to go easy on the mayo."

"Thank you, Sheriff Lennox," Linsy replied from her neatly organized desk.

He then turned his attention to Blue. "I wondered when you'd be back." His even tone made it sound as if he had been expecting her arrival. Worse, it almost sounded as if he thought Blue was late.

Blue stumbled over her sentence. "How did you know I'd be back?"

"You're a Wickam."

"What does that mean?"

Sheriff Lennox walked over to his desk and laughed, "I've known four generations of Wickam women. All creative and curious. Did you know that your great-grandmother is the reason the lighthouse was funded for so long?"

"I didn't."

"I thought you'd be back days ago. Better late than never." He definitely thought Blue was late.

"I have a hunch about the professor."

Mirth danced in Sheriff Lennox's gaze as he settled into the chair behind his desk. He handed Linsy a neatly wrapped sandwich and turned his attention back to Blue. "Let's hear it."

"What if the development company is working with the mayor to get the luxury apartment complex built?"

Sheriff Lennox leaned forward and tutted, "Water's wet. What else have you got?"

Blue opened and closed her mouth as she tried to bring up the next part of her mentally mapped conversation. Sheriff Lennox's attitude was simultaneously comforting and jarring. He arched a bushy brow as if waiting for Blue to continue. Sheriff Lennox opened his sandwich and took a generous bite.

She sucked in a deep breath and explained, "I think I can prove the professor was murdered by the development company."

Sheriff Lennox lowered his turkey sandwich and grinned. "Now we're getting somewhere."

Chapter 27

"I'm not sure if this is the best idea."

Charlie laughed as he readjusted the collar of his shirt. "It's the only idea which makes it the best idea."

"Only by default."

"What does your gut say?"

Checkmate.

Blue sighed, "My gut says that this is the best chance we have to get some answers before everyone votes on the development."

"See? We don't exactly have the luxury of time now that the entire town plans to vote on the development in the morning."

"Talk about cutting it close." Blue tapped her fingers against the side of her phone as the two waited inside Melinda's coffee shop. Melinda's shop accepted online orders so it was the perfect excuse to use a delivery service connected to an email.

The winding line of tourists reached outside of the door. The plan was simple. Charlie would convince the CEO to order food online. He'd be able to look over the

CEO's shoulder and confirm his email address while also applying pressure about the murder. Two birds with one stone. Easy.

Chapter 28

The plan was not easy. Blue wanted to hear every word between Charlie and his boss. Unfortunately, it seemed like she had accidentally settled for every fifth sentence. Her hiding spot inside of the supply closet was worse than she had thought.

The voices of excited tourists moved into the cramped space and pushed out the CEO's. Maybe Charlie and his boss hadn't started talking. Has the CEO even arrived? It wasn't like Blue would be able to tell from her secluded hiding spot.

Blue reached down and plucked her phone out of her front pocket. Her fingers glided over the screen as she quickly typed out a message.

BOSS HERE?

Blue figured it wasn't her best work, but it would get her point across. She waited a few seconds before her phone buzzed with an incoming message.

HE JUST ARRIVED. UPDATE SOON.

Blue had realized too late that the supply closet was surprisingly well-insulated. Even with the door partially cracked, she could only hear the customers directly outside of the space. Energy raced up and down Blue's spine as she anxiously waited for an update. She was glad Charlie had agreed to confront his boss in a crowded space. To Blue, Melinda's coffee shop was the safest safe haven in all of Shoreside.

Seconds moved into minutes. Blue shifted her feet as she impatiently waited to hear more. She stepped back and knocked into one of the shelves. A stack of clean towels landed on her head. Blue cursed as she tripped over a bottle of window cleaner. Her muscles tensed as she waited for someone to open the door and discover her presence. Eventually she realized either no one had heard or no one cared enough to check. Either reason worked for Blue.

She debated sitting on the floor, but the wayward buckets and mops threatened to topple to fall with the slightest movement. Resigned to her fate, Blue leaned against the partially opened door and tried her best to catch even the smallest fragment of the conversation.

After what felt like ages, light poured into the dim supply closet. Blue blinked her eyes as she stumbled out of the darkness. Charlie grinned as he reached out and steadied Blue.

A few customers looked over at the commotion as Blue accidentally kicked a mop across the floor. So much for being subtle. Melinda laughed from behind the counter but didn't make a move to stop the scene from unfolding.

Blue leaned into Charlie's gentle yet firm grip on her upper arm. She tilted her head to the side so she could see his features. "What did you find out?"

"I found out more than expected."

Blue huffed, "Now you sound like a riddle."

Charlie laughed as he walked over and retrieved the wayward mop. He returned it to the supply closet and closed the door.

"Bingo. I think we're left with more questions than answers."

Blue looked around the packed room and realized they needed to go somewhere more private to talk. She glanced at Melinda and noticed how her cousin was watching them like a hawk from behind the espresso maker. As if reading

Blue's mind, Melinda hollered, "You can use the backroom."

"Thanks, Melinda." Blue nodded as she walked around the counter and dodged behind a beaded curtain.

Charlie followed her lead. The two entered a shoebox-sized room. Blue flicked on the lava lamp placed in the corner of the room and inspected the stack of wayward CDs placed next to a CD player and an inflatable sofa. The room was Melinda's version of Blue's art studio. It meant a lot to Blue that her cousin trusted her to enter the private space. The lava in the lamp cast a faint glow over the room while the beaded curtain offered them some semblance of privacy. The coffee machines whirred at full volume and Blue felt comforted by the knowledge that they wouldn't be overheard. As soon as they were carefully tucked into the small space, Blue folded her hands across her waist and instructed, "Spill."

"He didn't do it."

Chapter 29

"What do you mean he didn't do it? I thought the threatening letter was sent from his email address?" Blue frowned as she listened to Charlie's newest update about the CEO.

All leads pointed to the CEO. He had the best reason for wanting the environmentalist removed from the picture. His company stood to make a massive profit as soon as the luxury development was approved and the wetlands were rezoned for housing. Two steps that appeared more likely to happen with each passing day. Who else stood to benefit from murdering the environmentalist?

Seeing her confusion, Charlie elaborated, "I thought it was him. He used the email address to order our food. I looked over and confirmed it was his email address. But I think someone used his email address to send the threat. Everyone in the office jokes that he's used the same three passwords since starting the company. I don't know the passwords, but I'm willing to bet that a few people do."

Charlie spoke quickly as he tried to convey as much information as possible. He needed to head back to his office in a few minutes to avoid looking suspicious. Not that many people would bother to question him after he just had lunch with the boss.

Blue nodded as understanding shifted her priorities, "So anyone in the company could have used the email?"

"Right."

Worry etched across Blue's face as she reconsidered, "Do you think he was suspicious about you asking questions?"

Charlie stared off into the lava lamp. He slowly shook his head, "No, I tried to bring it up casually but that meant I wasn't able to ask too many questions."

An incredulous snort escaped Blue, "You've asked enough."

Charlie wiggled his brows, "Were you worried about me?"

Warmth crept up the base of Blue's neck as she tried to maintain her calm. Unwilling to admit the full truth, she grumbled, "How could I not?"

The space between their bodies crackled with energy as they stood less than a few inches apart. Painfully close.

Blue wanted to close the distance between their bodies but she forced herself to take a small step back. She needed to focus on solving the mystery.

"How do you know the CEO didn't kill the environmentalist?"

Charlie cleared his throat and explained, "He didn't know the environmentalist was a man."

"What?"

"We were talking and he slipped up. He assumed the person found in the wetlands was a woman. Now, we both know that's wrong but he doesn't. Apparently, Sheriff Lennox hadn't given him much information. The CEO seems to think the body belonged to a woman."

A small smile inched along Blue's lips. While this wasn't exactly the information that she had hoped for, it was still a massive step in the right direction. Unfortunately, Blue struggled to think of another person who had the same level of motivation.

"Who else would have a large enough reason to kill the environmentalist?"

Charlie shrugged, "I guess that's what we need to find out."

The entire town was set to vote on the luxury development in the morning. Time was working against them and their window to catch the killer was getting smaller by the minute.

Uncertainty flitted through Blue's eyes as she tried to come up with another possible suspect. She knew there was an answer, but she just couldn't seem to find it.

Her voice sounded incredibly small as she murmured, "What if we're too late?"

Charlie grumbled, "Oh, no. You've gotten us this far. You put together the pieces about the wetlands and tied together a strong motive for the CEO. I hate to admit it, but I think someone from my company had to be involved. What is it that you always say?"

Blue hummed as she replied, "Sometimes it's hard to see the full picture when you're staring at a handful of brushstrokes. Maybe we need to take a step back."

"Exactly. Let's retrace our steps. We have almost a full day before the town votes on the development. Anything can happen between now and then."

Charlie's positive nature lifted Blue's spirit. She sucked in a deep breath and nodded. Wickam women never gave up. This was just a setback.

"What's our next move?"

Blue smiled, "I think it's back to the drawing board."

Chapter 30

The community center bustled with members of the Shoreside community. Blue looked around and spotted a few familiar faces that she hadn't seen in months.

Blue felt sick with worry. They were moments away from voting on the luxury development. She planned to make her case right before the vote. Not one for public speaking, Blue hoped her recent discoveries and data pulled from the archives would be enough to convince the crowd.

After the storm, the town seemed to come together. The atmosphere felt charged with energy as people spoke to family members and reconnected with old friends. The moment reminded Blue why her discovery was so important. She patted the phone tucked into the front pocket of her jeans and sighed. If only she had more time.

Sheriff Lennox hadn't found any more clues. He hovered near the back of the room as he observed the crowd with an impartial eye. Linsy stood to his right with a notebook in tow. She surveyed the onlookers and wrote down a few words from time to time.

The front row of the meeting was packed with suit-clad members of the development company. A few kids from the college's environmental club sulked against the back wall. They donned shirts encouraging people to vote in favor of saving the wetlands.

The mayor donned a sleek red suit and a patterned black tie. His presence earned a lukewarm round of applause as he approached the stage. The mayor clapped his hands above the microphone and the sound resounded from the speakers in a series of thunderous bangs. Blue covered her ears as the rest of the town groaned.

"Good to know the microphone works," Mayor Howard offered a grin that curled over his upper lip as he greeted the crowd. His slicked back hair shined against the harsh overhead lighting. He greeted, "Welcome Shoreside! I am so pleased to have us vote on this wonderful opportunity. In just a few moments, we will be able to vote on the development of an amazing luxury apartment complex. Don't worry, we will build the complex over the wetlands. The project won't go over any important land."

Blue rolled her eyes. Good thing the mayor wasn't biased.

The mayor shifted his weight as he added, "If anyone has any objections to this project, now is the time to speak."

Blue stepped down the aisle of plastic chairs and declared, "I object!"

Every pair of eyes in Shoreside turned in Blue's direction as she strode over to the stage.

Chapter 31

The mayor balked as Blue approached the stage. Clearly, he hadn't expected any pushback from the public. He blustered for a few seconds before a white toothy grin crept onto his face.

"This is what democracy is all about, folks. Belinda wants to make a point. Let's at least let her say her piece before we vote."

The mayor's belittling tone rubbed Blue the wrong way. It took every ounce of self-control in her body to avoid playing into the mayor's hand. She nodded and stepped closer to the microphone. The paintings and compiled graphs suddenly felt heavier in her hands.

Blue took a step forward and looked out over the crowd. Her eyes surveyed the curious faces as they waited for Blue to begin. She stood on the tips of her toes and pulled the microphone closer to her level. Satisfied, Blue decided there was no time like the present.

"Hello, my name is Belladonna but my friends call me Blue. Who am I kidding?

I'm pretty sure this entire room calls me Blue."

The injection of humor hit the mark. Laughter entered the room and put Blue's nerves at ease. She licked her lower lip and continued, "I have had the pleasure of living in Shoreside for all of my life. The recent storm put everything into perspective for me. We need the wetlands to ensure Shoreside lives on for the next generations. As many of you know, I'm from a family of artists. Three generations of Wickams have drawn this coastline and it's changed dramatically as we've removed portions of the wetlands."

Blue paused as she held up images of her grandmother's oil paintings. She then brought her own artwork out and allowed the crowd to compare the two side-by-side images.

"As you can see, the wetlands act as a natural barrier. It harbors all kinds of wildlife and also protects our town." She pointed to an area and continued, "The street that recently flooded was built over part of the wetlands. Here are a few charts that break down the information."

Murmurs escaped the crowd as people leaned forward and listened to Blue's explanation. The mayor shifted as if his feet were touching hot coals. He hovered behind Blue's back, but she didn't pay him any attention.

She observed the faces in the crowd which included friends she had known for years. They inspected the information with hushed voices and furrowed brows as if it was the first time that they had ever heard such news. Perhaps, because it likely was their first time.

Blue held her shoulders back and pressed, "The wetlands need to stay. Agreeing to the development is a short-term financial solution capable of creating long-term problems."

The mayor nudged Blue away from the microphone. She collected her charts and paintings as Mayor Howard ushered her away. Blue huffed, she hadn't finished her speech but she hoped it was enough to get the crowd thinking.

"Thank you for showing us your artistic theory," Mayor Howard narrowed his eyes at Blue. Instead of shrinking under the displeased stare, Blue stood taller and arched a single brow.

He folded his hands together and pushed, "I think it's time for a vote. We all know this is a completely safe proposal. I wouldn't consider any plan that wasn't completely safe."

Blue walked down the stage's stairs and found a spot a few paces away from the front row. The community center felt packed to the gills. Blue was grateful for the additional bodies that helped hide her from any curious stares.

"Okay, it's time to vote!"

"All in favor, raise your hands. Linsy will tally the votes."

Blue looked around the room and watched as the vote appeared to split down the middle. She counted the hands and frowned as the front row attempted to vote. They weren't locals. As soon as the thought crossed Blue's mind, Linsy corrected, "Please lower your hand's front row. You are not registered locals."

Bubbling laughter rang across the room and Blue noticed a few townspeople even lowered their hands after the comment. They sent the developers questioning gazes while Linsy recounted the vote.

Linsy pushed up her glasses and announced, "The vote for those in favor of the development has been tallied."

The mayor nodded, "Excellent. Let's count the votes against Shoreside's progress."

Blue raised her hand. She noticed a large pocket of the individuals standing around her also raised their hands. She tried to get a better look around the room but found it next to impossible with so many tall people blocking her view.

Linsy's clear voice rang out, "It's a tie."

Chapter 32

Blue had never considered a tie. What happened in the event of a tie? The townspeople erupted in commotion as the mayor attempted to regain control of the situation. He clapped his hands near the microphone and the unpleasant sound echoed through the speakers.

The crowd fell into a tumultuous silence. Blue stared at the mayor as he announced, "I guess this means that it's up to me to break the tie. He looked over to the people in the front row. Blue found it ironic that not a single person living in Shoreside was sitting in the front.

From the corner of her eyes, she noticed how one of the men in the front row motioned to the mayor. The hand gesture was so small that Blue almost assumed that she had imagined it. No, she stood taller and narrowed her eyes. The mayor imperceptibly dipped his head as if to reply to some unspoken request. The discovery threw a new theory into the works.

The mayor grinned like a cat after eating a canary. He inflected something that seemed to resemble remorse into his tone,

"It brings me no pleasure to have to cast the deciding vote. I believe in progress and I approve of the development."

"Not so fast!" A small woman with dark hair and glowing tanned skin stood from her seat. Her cool gaze stared down the mayor as if he were a fly in desperate need of swatting. Blue instantly recognized Myna Sage, the woman who had withdrawn from the mayoral race.

Myna steepled her fingers as her hardened gaze rested on Mayor Howard. She pushed, "The mayor is not allowed to have a vote during town meetings. It's considered a conflict of interest."

Blue smirked, she knew Myna was the real deal. The crowd grew unsettled as Mayor Howard grappled for control. Before he could say another word, Linsy added, "It's true. The mayor is not allowed to vote. It's a tradition that we take a break before revoting."

Mayor Howard's face looked flustered. His eyes narrowed into slits while his mouth opened into a biting smile. He hissed into the microphone, "Let's vote in 20 minutes. I'm sure we will all have come to our senses by then."

He stomped down the stairs in a fit of rage and escaped through the community center's backdoor. Blue watched as one of the men sitting in the front row stood and prepared to follow the mayor.

Blue refused to wait a second longer. She reached down and pressed the record button on her phone. She sprinted to catch up with the suit-wearing developer.

"Excuse me! Pardon me!" Blue weaved between bodies as the crowd parted. A few locals tried to congratulate her, but Blue was too focused on her mission to offer a proper response. Her heart raced as she stumbled to a stop just a few feet away from the man in a sleek gray suit. His dark eyes held a barely contained anger as he turned down his nose and barked, "What?"

"I know everything." Blue fibbed. She did not know everything, but the man in the expensive suit didn't need to know that.

Chapter 33

Blue agreed to meet with the man behind the stage. The red curtains hid them from sight. A chill raced down Blue's spine as she worried she'd just made a horrible mistake.

"What do you know?"

The crowd was so loud that it overpowered their conversation. While they were technically in the same room, it felt like a different universe. Blue gulped. She put on her sternest face as she hedged, "I know you bribed the mayor to push your development through."

A knowing look crossed the man's face. His nostrils flared but he kept silent. Blue knew she was right, but she needed him to admit it. Maybe she needed to raise the stakes. It was a stretch, but her gut knew that it was right.

She straightened her spine, "I know about the environmentalist."

Fury coated the man's tone, "You're digging your grave. If you were smart, you'd just leave this alone and go back to enjoying life in your little town. The last person that came poking around ended up drowning."

The pieces fell into place. The mayor was working with this stranger to approve the development. The mayor knew. Suddenly, Mayor Howard's weak excuses about protecting the Christmas Market's tourism made sense. He wanted to silence the news of the environmentalist's death to avoid drawing attention to his nefarious actions.

"You used your CEO's email to threaten Professor Matt. You lured him into the wetlands with the promise of a meeting."

"Close. Professor Matt was willing to recommend the development in exchange for a bribe. He needed money and was eager to sell out the wetlands, for a price. He was greedy and asked for too much."

Blue spluttered as she took a small step back, "So you killed him?"

The stranger chuckled as he towered over Blue. He growled as his once controlled anger crumbled and gave way to rage. "Do you know who does all of the hard work for this company? Me. I make the budget cuts and coordinate the key investor meetings. Not the person who uses less than three variations of his wife's name for passwords."

Blue took a step back as she tried to stall. She knew the space was too cumbersome to navigate. Would she be able to push through the thick stage curtains before the man grabbed her? It looked like she was about to find out.

Her voice came out calmer than expected as she pushed, "So you know the CEO's passwords?"

"Know them? I helped him set them up. I do the dirty work to protect the company. He's too soft. Always has been and always will be. It's time to take the company and this town in a different direction."

Blue squealed as the man in the gray suit pounced. She unlocked the small pepper spray and aimed the canister in his direction.

In the blink of an eye, Charlie appeared and tackled Blue's would-be attacker to the ground. The pepper spray wafted through the air and Blue took a few steps back to escape the potent chemicals. Charlie didn't even notice. He was too busy overpowering the man in the gray suit.

"Charlie! If you help me, I'll make you the new VP of Finance."

"I never liked your job, Smith!" Charlie hissed as he flatted the man named Smith against the stage's wooden floor.

The commotion intensified as a group of townspeople lifted the velvet curtains. They easily hefted the stranger onto his feet. Sheriff Lennox chuckled as he cuffed the rogue developer.

"You can't prove anything! Charlie, you're fired!" Tears leaked from the man's reddened eyes as he spluttered a string of unintelligible curses.

Sheriff Lennox roughly checked the handcuffs attached to the man's wrists. Satisfied, he whistled, "Good job, Charlie. You should consider working for the force."

The backstage area thrummed with commotion and Blue stayed quiet as she took in the scene. She recognized every person who had come to her aid. Sheriff Lennox and a few local fishermen carted the stranger away. Charlie's eyes tracked their departure before he sped over to Blue. His red eyes anxiously searched her face for any sign of harm.

"Are you hurt? What happened? Did he touch you?"

Blue sucked in a shaky breath, "No, I'm fine. You tackled him right before anything happened."

Charlie grumbled as he gently cupped the side of Blue's face. The collar of his cable knit sweater was ripped down the middle. His usually well-combed hair stood out in every direction as red tinged the corners of his eyes. But given the circumstances, he looked no worse for wear.

"I was almost too slow."

Blue frowned, "Your eyes. The pepper spray got in your eyes."

Charlie guffawed, "That's what you're choosing to focus on? I'll buy you another pepper spray."

"I'm not upset about the pepper spray, I'm upset it got in your eyes. Let's get you some milk."

Blue guided them down the side stairs that connected the back of the stage to the mouth of the community center. Blue poked her head out of the hallway and instructed Amanda to grab her a glass of milk. Amanda didn't ask a single question. She returned with a glass of milk and sped back into the sea of people. It was obvious Amanda had seen the developer hauled away in cuffs and connected the dots.

Blue and Charlie stayed tucked into the small hallway as they indulged in a private moment. Blue dipped the napkin into the milk and carefully dabbed Charlie's face. She hummed in discontent as she got to work on soothing his irritated skin.

"How did you know I was with him?"

A smile creased the corners of Charlie's lips as he admitted, "I kept you in my sight. I knew trouble would find you."

Blue laughed, "Really?"

"Yes, it also helped that you called me."

"I did?"

Blue frowned as she reached into her pocket and pulled out her phone. Sure enough, her phone said that she was still on a call with Charlie.

"Sorry, I'm still getting used to having a phone on me."

Charlie shrugged, "At least you used it."

Blue looked over Charlie's face and whispered, "Can I tell you a secret?"

"What?"

"I think you're really good at interpreting the spirit of the law."

Charlie laughed before he winced.

"Very funny, Blue."

Chapter 34

Strings of Christmas lights covered the rooftops along Heart Street. Every window display detailed a festive scene. Blue nestled into her red coat as she admired the newest additions to the local art gallery. The added notes of color made her newest oil painting pop. While she'd only had time to finish one, it was enough to generate excitement for her upcoming collection. Pride filled Blue's chest as she overheard tourists and neighbors alike, complimenting her unique style.

Amanda waved Blue to come closer. She walked to the back of the gallery and noticed a slender woman in a sleek gold dress standing next to Amanda. The woman looked oddly familiar.

Amanda smiled, "Just the person I was hoping to see. Blue meet Blithe. Blithe is a top curator for personal art collections. One of her clients would love to purchase a few pieces from your upcoming collection."

"That's amazing. Does your client have anything in mind?"

Blithe smiled and her intelligent eyes scanned Amanda and Blue as if she was the only one who knew a dazzling little secret. She replied, "Yes, he's particularly interested in your new collection. Here's my card."

Once Blithe exited the gallery, Amanda released a throaty laugh. "I think we just made it to the big leagues."

"I don't understand."

Amanda squeezed Blue's hand. "Whatever you're doing, keep doing it. Blithe is very well-connected and can put you into contact with amazing art collectors."

Blue joked, "Aren't you afraid of telling me this? Won't that potentially hurt your sales?"

Amanda lazily waved her hand in the air. She pointed at Blue, "I am a friendship-first kind of business owner. Blithe is a good connection. Besides, I'm not afraid of elevating your name. The more exposure you have to your name, the higher the prices for your art."

Blue laughed as she gave Amanda a large hug. A familiar towering figure appeared at Blue's side and offered her a glass of champagne. Charlie looked between the two women and asked, "Am I missing something?"

"Nothing you don't already know. Blue's art keeps getting better and better."

The gallery attendees moved around the trio positioned in the center of the floor. The trio talked for a few more minutes before Blue yawned and decided to explore the rest of the Christmas Market.

Charlie and Blue waved goodbye to Amanda as they exited the gallery and walked to the center of Heart Street. Food and activity booths lined both sides of the street. For the next week, the street belonged to the jovial vendors. With Christmas less than two days away, the market thrummed with talented street performers and delicious fair food.

"Where are we going?"

Blue laughed, "You'll see."

The duo reached the small park near the end of the street. A massive unlit Christmas tree sat in the center of the usually unsuspecting greenery. Mayor Myna stood near the base of the tree alongside Sheriff Lennox. A large crowd gathered around as Mayor Myna prepared to light the tree. Her right hand hovered over an intricately designed button.

Charlie smirked, "A tree lighting ceremony?"

"Yep. The Christmas Market is even better than the old mayor predicted."

"I still don't understand how Howard managed to beat Myna."

Blue kept her eyes on the tree as she replied, "Turns out he cheated. His brother helped tally the votes."

"Talk about a conflict of interest."

"You're telling me."

"I think Myna brings more taste to the position. Speaking of taste, I've been thinking." Charlie hesitated as his voice lingered on the last few words of his sentence.

"About what?"

Charlie coughed, "You inspire me, Blue. You reinvented yourself and that took courage. I decided to do something similar."

Blue pushed her blonde locks away from her face as she took a better look at Charlie's face. His gentle eyes held a barely contained secret.

She playfully nudged Charlie's side, "I think we've had enough mysteries to last us until the end of the year. What are you talking about? Spill the beans."

"I've decided to leave my job and start my own company. I spent so long looking for reasons to stay that I forgot to

consider the reasons why I deserve to leave.
I want to take a chance on myself."

"That's amazing. Didn't the CEO offer you a promotion after catching the VP of Finance?"

Charlie deadpanned, "I tackled the VP of Finance."

"You know what I mean," Blue narrowed her eyes.

"I do. Yes, he offered me a raise and a promotion. But it just didn't feel like the place for me. Besides, I already have my first client."

Blue's brows shut up into her hairline as surprise colored her features. "Oh?"

Satisfaction danced across Charlie's face as he looked at Blue and winked. He then straightened his back and made eye contact with Mayor Myna. The mayor noticed the duo standing in the crowd and waved. Blue's jaw slackened as she put together the clues.

"Your first client is Mayor Myna?"

"Close, my first client is the city of Shoreside. The city hired me to go over their zoning policies which could take me a while seeing as they're outdated and mostly written on paper."

"I see, so you'll be staying in Shoreside?"

The two leaned closer. Blue stood on the tips of her toes as Charlie leaned down. Charlie breathed a single word against Blue's lips, "Indefinitely."

Red and white Christmas lights sparked into existence as Mayor Myna lit the tree. The crowd hooted and hollered while Charlie and Blue remained silent. They were too busy saying everything that they meant to each other with a lingering tender kiss.

Chapter 35

"Thank you for walking me home, Charlie. You know it's no longer necessary now that Mayor Howard and your previous company's VP of Finance are in jail."

Charlie tutted, "I don't have to walk you home. I want to walk you home, Blue."

"Always the gentleman."

"I'm still trying to make up for my first impression."

Blue laughed, "Consider it forgiven."

The two took the long way home and cut down the road that paralleled the wetlands. Egrets bathed in the cool fresh water while crickets happily chirped in the distance. Blue gazed at the natural beauty as a deep sense of peace washed over her.

A shiny new sign stood at the entrance of the greenery. Blue frowned as she wandered over to the plaque. Had the wetlands ended up getting sold to the developers after all?

Disappointment danced in Blue's gut as she inched closer to the sign. What if everything she did was wasted? She stepped closer and struggled to read the sign against the glare of the waning sun.

She murmured, "Was it rezoned?"

Charlie shrugged, "Something like that."

The duo approached the newly resurrected plaque. Gold letters spelled out a familiar name. "Professor Matt's Wetlands Reserve."

Tears pricked the back of Blue's eyes as she turned her attention back to Charlie. She rubbed her palm over her chest and mumbled, "You did this?"

"It was my idea. Mayor Myna expedited the project. Professor Matt's memory doesn't need to be defined by a bad choice made in his final moments. The wetlands are officially rezoned and protected."

Blue leaped into Charlie's arms before he could finish his sentence. The duo stumbled back a few steps before Charlie regained his balance.

A throaty chuckle rumbled against Blue's cheek. Charlie stroked the side of Blue's face as he admitted, "I couldn't think of a better first project for my company."

Blue pulled her head away from Charlie's chest and whispered, "Can I tell you a secret?"

"Anything."

Blue pressed closer to Charlie's chest and inhaled his woodsy scent. "I think you're trying to seduce me."

Charlie smiled as leaned down and gently pressed his lips against Blue's forehead. "Is it working?"

"I guess you'll need to solve that mystery on your own. Walk me home."

Thank you for reading
A Very Coastal Christmas:

Thank you for reading another novel within the wonderful Cozy Christmas series! I massively appreciate that you took the time to read my book. As a small indie author, every review helps.

I love hearing from readers while building a mystery-focused community. Thank you for reading small and thinking big!

Review Link:

http://amazon.com/review/create-review?&asin=B0D75VWZSB

CAMILLE CABRERA'S BOOKS:

Catalina's Tide
The Rule of Three
The Mystery of Mistletoe Motel
Chronometer
Our Perfect Murder
Lady Cavendish's Christmas Caper
Below the Water
The First Paper Cut: An Anniversary to Die For
Troublesome Trades: The Inkblot Crow Mystery
Troublesome Trades: Discovering the Glass Queen
Troublesome Trades: The Glass Slipper
Troublesome Trades: Crime Always Pays
Troublesome Trades: Feathers and Fate
Delivered
Broadcasting Christmas Cheer
A Very Coastal Christmas
Below Boston

CAMILLE CABRERA

Camille Cabrera is a #1 bestselling American mystery author. She specializes in sub genres including noir and cozy mystery. Her works often involve complicated and controversial female protagonists. She takes great pride creating works that revolve around a specific holiday to contrast the familiar celebration with the unknown shroud of death.

Cabrera's first Christmas mystery, THE MYSTERY OF MISTLETOE MOTEL, previously reached the number one spot on Amazon's Mystery Romance chart. LADY CAVENDISH'S CHRISTMAS CAPER ranked within the top 10 on four different Amazon charts during its debut month.

THE MYSTERY OF MISTLETOE MOTEL

Promising accountant Lacy Pondwater never wanted to own the Mistletoe Motel. However, when Lacy's mother passes away and her dad grows too old to readjust roof tiles, she scrambles, with the help of her younger sister Stacy, to keep the family business afloat. On a constantly shrinking shoestring budget, Lacy's maxed out every credit card and is at the end of her rope.

After a few too many glasses of wine and paranormal crime shows, Lacy embellishes the description of the Mistletoe Motel online to include Victorian era haunts and the occasional ghost encounter.

A question slowly circles around the back of Lacy's mind. Did she inadvertently invite a haunting to Mistletoe Motel, or are her eager guests merely manifesting their own adventures? Of course, white lies always come back to bite, and when a ghost hunting television show asks to film, the sisters reluctantly agree. Only a Christmas miracle can save the motel from bankruptcy and Lacy from a life of fraud.

THE MYSTERY OF MISTLETOE MOTEL

CHAPTER 1 TEASER…

"Dang it!" The expletive rolled from my tongue as steam nearly poured from my ears. My temper was about to erupt. The only thing holding back my verbal eruption of epic proportions was the tiniest bit of patience that I'd haphazardly taped back together, just like every single pipe and banister inside of our crumbling motel.

Stacy was so busted. How many times had I told her to make sure the meat locker was closed? How many times had I politely opened and closed it in front of her doe-eyed stare in the hopes that at least one lightbulb would turn on in that willfully empty house of a brain? Too many. Now, she was so dead. Well, more figuratively than literally. She was my younger sister, after all.

Of course, I knew that I wasn't being fair. Stacy had a great heart with a wonderfully vibrant open mind, but sometimes her attempts at helpfulness really made it difficult to keep the motel afloat. Her real calling was instructing yoga classes in an outdoor setting surrounded by vibrant people and my real calling was
hiding behind piles of papers dotted with tiny numbers.

Unfortunately, both of our dreams were currently put on hold for the greater purpose of saving the legacy that our parents had left us. It felt like I'd mentally carved out a room in my mind for accounting and simply got up and left the next day. I hadn't even settled into the role for a full day before saving the family business rightly took priority. Maybe once everything has settled I could one day follow along as Stacy teaches a yoga class. Until then, we were stuck working together with tensions beyond high and stress levels operating at maximum capacity.

We weren't always like this. I shook away the thoughts from another time and snapped back to the moment. A new fresh wave of anxiety masked as fear zipped through my bloodstream.

I could just picture Stacy's slim arms folded over her chest as her statuesque features turned shocked and tinged with embarrassment. I angrily stomped around the piles of ruined meat products. The gene pool had played the opposite card with me. It had graciously provided me with all of the potential to be an excellent accountant as well as all of the love of pastries to also be in competition with the Pillsbury Doughboy. At least, that's how I felt living through

my early teens and rougher-than-needed
middle school years in a small town. It was
something that had really bothered me in my
youth, but nearly a decade later, it now
meant that I enjoyed my little dimples and
curves in a way that younger me would
take ten years to fully understand.

The slight stench told me the meat was bad,
but that didn't stop the dreamer in me from
personally inspecting every single thawed
rib-eye by hand. The earliest risers in the
motel were about to get up and the Mistletoe
Motel had no viable meat options for our
widely broadcasted continental breakfast. It
was a tradition from our parents that Stacy
and I had yet to throw away. No matter how
costly. Sentiments were expensive.

In all honesty, we only had a single room
booked and that was still more than our
usual occupancy rate. The real problem was
that we no longer had any meat for ourselves
or any future potential guests. A girl could
dream of the latter.

Worse still, we had no viable meat for
breakfast, lunch, or dinner for the next week.
That was a more realistic hurdle. I rubbed
my face in agitation as my messy mop of
brown hair remained barely restrained
by a threadbare hairband. I ran my tongue
over my

slightly crooked bottom teeth and felt the worn grooves and ridges. I had planned to get them straightened after college, but that was no longer in the cards for now. The bottom teeth were pushed together like a hungry shark. The dentist had said that the enamel would likely slowly erode if left untreated. I had laughed until tears had threatened to fall at the literal metaphor for the state of the motel that now resided on the inside of my mouth. It was a visible fixer-upper and a ticking time bomb of repercussions that was just waiting to explode.

Not that I minded. Well, maybe I did care and that's why this meat-locker-gate was just the perfect excuse to release some steam.

Two flights of well-worn cream carpeted stairs later and I huffed, hunched over, directly outside of Stacy's room. My long fingers rapped against the wooden door as I called, "Stacy, get up, you murderer! The meat locker was left open and everything inside has gone bad. I need to go shopping for food. Please watch the front desk!"

Lady Cavendish's Christmas Caper

CHAPTER 1 TEASER...

Flames hungrily licked around the burnt edges as angry dark spots marred the once pristine surface. Charlie instinctively knew all was lost. She had ruined the triple-layer bean casserole.

Clouds of smoke swirled around the kitchen as Charlie opened the ancient windows of her rustic Montana cabin. A fresh breeze rolled into the tiny abode and granted her a momentary reprieve from the smelly mess. She didn't have enough money to run out to the store and replace the charred dinner. It didn't help that the nearest store was nearly an hour away by car. The recipe had seemed simpler online.

Like usual, easier said than done.

Defeated, Charlie grumbled into the air "I guess a microwave dinner will do."

She cleaned up the kitchen and triple-checked that the small blaze had gone out. The remnants of the casserole resembled congealed plastic. She poured a cup of water onto the mess, just to be safe. With Charlie's luck, anything was possible. It wasn't exactly like she was living the high life, running between her job at the sports bar and her part-time gig at the mall. She was exhausted and too strapped for cash to spring for a pizza. She wondered what it would feel like to have enough loose pocket change to buy a pizza after an unfortunate kitchen accident. The prospect of a few extra dollars felt as foreign as an international vacation.

A commotion near the front door suddenly commanded Charlie's attention. She grabbed the nearest item within reach and held it up. The wooden serving spoon did little to boost Charlie's confidence as she crept closer to the locked door. An odd thick packet had landed on her wooden floor. The mail slot's cover swung back and forth from the force of the recent gift. Charlie looked down and noticed a bright red stamp that indicated a priority delivery. The parcel already commanded Charlie's full attention. She did not work in a field or live in an environment that called for any remotely time-sensitive deliveries.

Her curiosity got the best of her. She reached down and inspected the item. Charlie noticed the foreign postage and assumed it was a gift from her loving, mischievous grandmother. The two hadn't spoken in a little over a month. Wi-Fi was spotty living near the Rocky Mountains. The intense rainstorms only added to the typically temperamental connection.

A pile of assumptions jostled around in the back of Charlie's mind. Maybe her grandma had finally received her belated Christmas gift. Charlie knew that it wasn't her proudest moment. The gift was over a week late, but she tried.

Unconvinced the package belonged to her, Charlie double-checked the address. The package proudly stated it was intended for Charlotte Cavendish.

Charlie wrinkled her nose as she read her real name. Sure, Charlotte was a gorgeous name, but it just didn't fit. Charlottes were sophisticated and had plans. And Charlie, well, she was happy when she made a casserole without setting off the smoke detectors. She felt more like a Charlie. In her mind, a Charlie was still deciding where to go while a Charlotte was already driving full speed ahead.

Charlie slid her finger down the side of the thick envelope. She unfolded the sheets and read the first paragraph. Her mouth hung open in surprise. The letter was requesting her presence at the reading of Lady Cavendish's will.

Charlie itched her nose and wondered, "Who is Lady Cavendish?"

Broadcasting Christmas Cheer

CHAPTER 1 TEASER

People bustled out of the shop almost as quickly as they came in. The crowd moved around the bakery in droves while Madison sat in silence. Watching.

"Aren't you happy you moved to Lakewood? You'll never find another town with tastier strudel."

Angie proudly held up her half-chomped pastry and clinked it against the side of Madison's steaming cup of hot chocolate.

Madison's smile didn't fully reach her coffee-colored eyes as she gave her new friend a half-hearted smile.

"Yes, I never had a snack like this in New York. To be fair, I rarely went out for a bite to eat in the city. Who knew that I needed to move all the way to Colorado to find such an awesome family-run place?"

"Sweetie's Bakery is the gift that keeps on giving. I hope the new bakery down the street knows what they've gotten into. This town has a competitive food scene that runs several generations deep. Sweetie's Bakery is a town favorite. Anyways, don't worry,

Madison. It's normal to feel homesick after such a large move; especially so close to the holidays. Besides, you've barely been here a month. It's going to take a little time for you to feel settled!"

Madison winced, "I moved here six months ago."

"Already?"

Angie swallowed her last bite. Her pearly award-winning smile glimmered in the cheerful sunlight as she added, "Time flies when most of your life is work. It's hard to find the time when you're a news reporter in a small town, but you'll get used to it. If you think about it, the holidays are chaotic wherever you move. Let's see how you feel by the start of the new year."

The bakery's location was originally an old home. The 1800s home was recently converted into one of the most popular shops in town. Apparently, the bakery has outgrown its previous location. Madison's brown orbs took in the dining area. The owner preserved the structure's old-world charm and embraced the massive wooden pillars. She saw the vision. A vision that made it difficult to find a better place to grab a snack. Madison loved that the bakery offered free pastries at the end of the day. Who knew giving away day-old pastries could be such a genius way to avoid food waste?

Madison hummed in the back of her throat. If the new bakery was even half as delicious as this one, she was in for a treat. Literally.

Still, she didn't like feeling left out. Angie seemed so settled into the motions of her daily life. Madison wondered if she could have something like that in the future. A future that seemed to be slipping through Madison's fingers by the minute. After six months, all Madison had to show for her move across the country was a winding list of text messages between her and her not-so-new boss.

"What's the name of the new bakery?"

Angie covered her mouth as she spoke over a pile of pastry, "I think it starts with the letter A."

"Angel?"

"Something like that."

The kind words bolstered Madison's courage as she leaned back against the wooden chair. Patrons of the tiny bakery bustled near the front of the store. Madison had to hand it to them, Sweetie's Bakery definitely had a reputation. Upbeat music charged the air as customers came and went through the front door. Luckily, the people behind the counter seemed to be pros at getting people where they needed to go.

Madison soaked in the bakery's atmosphere as Angie reached for her second pastry. Large green and red ornaments hung from cheerful garlands wrapped around the exposed wooden rafters while twinkle lights cast the room in a soft glow.

Angie pulled out her phone between bites and snapped a photo of the elaborate decorations. Madison shot her friend a curious glance.

"What? You don't like taking photos?"

Madison shrugged, "I haven't really felt the need to take any pictures. I like to take photos whenever something feels important."

"How many pictures have you taken since moving here? Before you say anything, work-related photos don't count."

Madison balked, "We don't know if I was about to include work photos. Let me see."

She made a big show of opening her phone and searching through her photos, only to be sadly disappointed. Three images. Two of

those photos she'd snapped and sent to her
parents to show off her cozy new place.
She'd been so proud of her new home just
inside of the forest. The owners had even
included the furniture. The third photo in her
camera roll? Oh, that didn't count. She'd
taken a photo of the promising new skate
park for an upcoming assignment.
The Lakewood community sure loved to
skate.

"I see your point, Angie."

Angie hummed in acknowledgment and
swallowed another generous gulp of her
drink. Madison enjoyed the rare occasion
when her mind could move away from
work-isolated sentiments. Maybe she did
need to make more of an effort to fit in. The
realization popped her previous excitement
like a bright balloon brushing against a
sewing needle.

Madison found it impossible to feel down
for long when surrounded by such an upbeat
atmosphere. She looked around the room
and realized Angie was the only familiar
face.

"You're right, I did jump in. But sometimes
I worry that I jumped headfirst. Working as
a news reporter right out of school is
amazing. To be fair, I did take my time
going back to school. My gap year before

getting my master's degree accidentally
turned into three. Having this job so quickly
after getting out of school is my dream come
true. I guess I'm still eager to prove that I
deserve this job. I'm still not sure how to fit
a personal life alongside my career."

Angie pushed, "There's no time like the
present to try and make that balance
happen."

COZY CHRISTMAS SERIES:

The Mystery of Mistletoe Motel

Lady Cavendish's Christmas Caper

Broadcasting Christmas Cheer

A Very Coastal Christmas

9 798218 567743